CLAY

CLAY

Melissa Harrison

WINDSOR
PARAGON

First published 2013
by Bloomsbury Publishing Plc
This Large Print edition published 2013
by AudioGO Ltd
by arrangement with
Bloomsbury Publishing Plc

Hardcover   ISBN: 978 1 4713 2643 1
Softcover   ISBN: 978 1 4713 2644 8

British Library Cataloguing in Publication Data available

Printed and bound in Great Britain by
MPG Books Group Limited

For Anthony

PROLOGUE

The little wedge-shaped city park was as beautiful and as unremarkable as a thousand others across the country, and despite the changing seasons many of the people who lived near it barely even knew that it was there—although that was certainly not true of all.

Once much larger, it had been designated common land back in Victorian times, a place 'for the enjoyment of all', but had been eaten into and built upon over the years, as is the way with land not seen to earn its keep. Now it was more like a very wide verge which followed the long, unlovely high road for much of its length, interrupted here and there by side streets and a few grander buildings which had fenced off their own stretch to make a private garden in defiance of planning laws nobody seemed willing to enforce.

The Plestor Estate formed its westernmost boundary and the bus-thundered high road its east. Along the high road were shops: nail bars, chicken parlours, newsagents, mobile phone unlocking, cheap calls to Africa, launderettes, cab offices and discount booze. Further out were street after street of terraces, some Edwardian, set on wide, tree-lined roads, some narrower and more crowded. There were tall housing blocks, too, and more estates, and to the east there were sidings and sheds and acres of shining track.

A few streets to the north-west were the broad open spaces of a common, many times bigger than the little park and bisected both by the railway line

1

and a road. Its grassy acres were big enough for football pitches and stately plane trees and shabby tennis courts and some surprisingly old oak woods that ran along the embankment on both sides.

The park, the common, the high road: it wasn't an area you could give a name to, or even a postcode; its borders were too intangible for that. Thousands passed through it every day with barely a glance, their lives intersecting in ways that they would most likely never come to know.

It was the rough territory of a dog fox; the distance an old lady with a stick could cover in an afternoon; the area a small boy could come to know and call his own.

1

ST BARTHOLOMEW'S DAY

The room was square and beige, with posters of lakes and snowy peaks on the walls and a box of old toys in the corner. There were two sofas with ill-fitting blue covers, and a rectangular table, bare except for a box of tissues and with two plastic chairs facing each other across it; two more were stacked in the corner. In the door was a window set with reinforced glass; the only window, in fact, in the whole room. Below the ceiling hung two small cameras with glowing red eyes.

A boy sat on one sofa holding a toy dog like he didn't know what to do with it. It was clear somebody had put it into his hands. Somebody well meaning; but he was ten now, too old for soft toys. He put it gently on the floor by his feet and pushed his hands between his knees. Kept his eyes on it.

On the other sofa was a young woman with large gold earrings and folded arms. She looked towards the boy, but not at him. Her expression, her posture, gave very little away. An older woman sat at the table, sorting through some papers in a folder. She looked up at the boy and at his mother, then put the folder away, down by the side of the table, as though there it might be somehow defused.

'All right then, TC,' she said. 'It says here that's what you like to be called, is that right?'

The boy glanced up at her briefly, then away.

'TC. Now you know you're not in any trouble,

don't you? You're not in any trouble at all.'

The boy nodded.

'Good. And you understand I'm not a policewoman?'

Again, he nodded. 'You're the social.'

'I work for social services, yes, that's right. Now, what I want to do today is find out a little bit about your friendship with Mr Łopata—with Jozef. Is that all right?'

'Is he in trouble?'

'Let's not worry about him for now, OK? For now I just want to build up a picture of what life's been like for yourself, OK, TC, and about how you came to know Jozef. Now, I understand that last September, soon after you started Year Five, you started missing school, is that right? Can you tell me why that was?'

* * *

It was hard for TC to remember everything that had happened a whole year ago. Such a lot of time had passed. He tried to think back to last September, before his mum started seeing Jamal, before he found the secret garden. Before he met Jozef.

* * *

TC had taken a book into school on the first day of Year Five. It was one of only two books he owned—although the other one was a secret.

This one he had stolen from a plastic crate outside a charity shop during the summer holidays. It was called *The Supernatural* and was full of grainy black-and-white photographs showing pots and pans sent flying through old-fashioned kitchens by poltergeists, cheery adventurers waving from the steps of planes that had later disappeared into thin air and religious statues weeping tears of human blood. Once he got it home he'd found he could not escape from its terrifying pull; that night it was as if all the terrors on its pages might burst out of it and fly howling around the room.

Since then he had allowed himself to look at it only in daylight, and he always made sure to close the covers firmly and hide it away before dark. Nevertheless, when he woke in the night his mind was often drawn back to the lurid pictures and the chilling text; he both wanted to know, and didn't want to know, how the world worked and whether it really was so treacherous.

He took it to school because he'd wanted Year Five to be different. He'd thought the book might bring him kudos of some kind, and pictured himself besieged by curious and admiring children, but as he stood in the playground with it on the first day of term, held mutely open at the most terrifying page, he found it earned him only mockery and jeers. He should have known better, he thought; as if that was ever going to work. Why did he have to keep on trying, why did he have to keep making it worse?

His other book had been bought for him by his father, although you could say he'd stolen that one, too. TC had not seen his dad for nearly three months, not since his mum kicked him out just before his ninth birthday, which wasn't fair. After all the shouting, after the sound of his feet on the echoing stairwell had died away—as it turned out for the last time—TC had watched from his

5

bedroom window as his mum took everything to do with his dad out to the bins far below, even the presents left wrapped and ready for TC's birthday. They were for him—for *him*; and he knew he would never forgive her.

That was the first time he left the flat at night by himself, creeping down the four flights of stairs with their buzzing, unreliable lights and overcoming untold horrors to reach blindly into the bin's black maw. There was only one present he could reach, and he opened it in secret in his bed that night—not that the secrecy was warranted, looking back, because from what he could tell his mother had hardly been into his room since then anyway.

The book was a guide to tracking wild animals, and since then TC had looked at it every single day. As well as the prints animals' feet left in mud and snow, it showed how to tell if a hazelnut had been nibbled by a squirrel or a mouse, what sorts of animals lived in what kinds of homes, and how to recognise different types of animal droppings. Instantly, TC knew why his dad had chosen it for him: they had watched survival programmes together, and his dad was going to teach him bushcraft. He'd been in the army—well, the Territorials, which was the same thing—and he knew everything about survival. They were going to go camping in the summer, although that would never happen, now.

His dad had chosen well, despite it really being a book for grown-ups. The parts TC didn't understand he pored over endlessly, and by the start of Year Five he knew what a herbivore was, if not the difference between 'your' and 'you're'; and he could roughly describe the distribution of water

6

voles across the country, although he did not yet know where any major cities were on a map.

Not that it counted for anything. The teachers weren't bothered if you knew about stuff like that, and the other kids certainly didn't care; they were all into football and Wii games and stuff. So at lunchtime on that first day back, having understood how it was to be, he did what he had been doing all summer long and simply took himself away: away to the little park where only the magpies scolded him from the trees, away to the common's grassy acres and the friendly oak woods at its margins; away to where he felt less alone. In the weeks without his father those few nondescript city acres—the park by the Plestor Estate, the common and the few godforsaken corners of scrub between the estate and the high road—had become overlaid with the landmarks of all his solitary imaginings, until every tree and fence post and path and thicket was charged with an almost mystical significance. The book had been the key: it showed him a secret world that existed alongside the daily, humdrum one, but that seemed invisible to most people. The birds weren't just things flapping about in the background; they had lives, just like people did: they got married, had families, fought each other and died, and so did the foxes and the squirrels and everything else. And it was happening all the time and all around him, not just in TV programmes, or in Africa or wherever. It was all going on, secretly and without anything to do with people; and TC longed, *longed*, to belong to it all.

And so, when the school bell rang for the end of lunch on the first day back, he was more than a mile away on the common, high in the branches of his

7

favourite oak. It had a friendly lower branch, then a satisfying scramble to the next level; then a choice: he could either sit with his back against the rough, reassuring trunk, or further out, in the crux of two tortuous branches, where dog walkers would often pass directly below, never suspecting the small boy sitting quietly above them. There, TC had carefully tied one slim twig in a loose knot. One day it would be a proper branch, and only he would know how it had come by its odd shape.

It didn't feel like autumn yet, it still felt like summer. The oak's leaves were still green, although some of the horse chestnuts were starting to turn; TC looked around and tried to imagine the thick canopy down on the ground and all the branches bare, but it didn't seem possible.

He thought about when his dad would come back, and how he could tell him everything he had learned. He would show him the bent grasses and scuffed earth that marked the place where a fox pushed its way under the fence by the station sidings night after night, or the empty, teardrop-shaped nest of a long-tailed tit, painstakingly woven from cobwebs and lichen and hair. Or perhaps by then he would have found his holy grail: an owl pellet, packed with fur and feathers and tiny bones that could be picked out and sorted to show what the owl had eaten. The tracking book said there weren't any owls in the city, but it also said there weren't very many foxes, and that definitely wasn't true. After all, there was a date in it telling when it had been published, and it was back when TC was just a baby, which left lots of time for owls to come. Perhaps one day he would hear one, and follow the sound to its roost, and below the roost would be the dry, regurgitated pellets: little gifts for his father, when he came home.

*   *   *

Apart from the time his mum dialled 999, it was TC's first real brush with the police. Hunger drove him down from the oak but he hadn't thought how it would look, a boy wandering around in uniform on a school day. When the two policemen called him over on Leasow Road he didn't even think to run away.

'How old are you, son?' asked the taller of the two.

'Nine.'

'And is that an Elmsford's uniform?'

TC's chest thumped, and his stomach dropped like a stone.

'And why aren't you in school today?'

He didn't have any answers; yet there was something about the man's hand on his shoulder as they steered him towards the high-rise blocks that felt almost like relief.

The coppers didn't like the lift not working. TC had to follow them at their pace up the stairs, their shoes black and ugly on each step, their trousers shiny and ill-fitting as school uniforms. They spoke to one another on the way up as though TC wasn't there.

At the fourth floor they stopped. 'This it, then?' TC wasn't even nervous now, not really bothered about what she might say. Something to get through, that was all. And then he could go to his room and look at his book.

But when she answered the door there was

9

someone standing behind her—a man was standing behind her. TC thought for one heart-thudding moment that it was his father, but that was stupid, this man was taller and darker, different, this man was not his father, not his father at all.

2

MICHAELMAS

In the mornings she would sit by the kitchen window and watch the early-morning dog walkers not picking up after their dogs. Then would come the commuters on their way to work and the parents taking their kids to school, using the little park outside her window as a short cut to the bus stop and dropping cigarette ends into the grass. All so young, and no idea of it! Still, she wouldn't want to be their age again. Too much to worry about. All the wrong things, too.

It was the end of September, and autumn was in the air. It had been a crisp weekend, brisk breezes chasing clouds across a blue sky and sending sycamore leaves down onto the grass where they would scud about for weeks, eventually forming a dry tide against the chain-link fence through which Sophia now looked and which marked the back boundary of the park. The Plestor Estate had been smart in the sixties and was ugly now, rain and grime staining its white render like tears, but her view of the trees was worth every deprivation that had befallen it since she and her late husband

Henry had bought their ground-floor flat, brand new, in 1961.

How wonderful it had seemed when they had first moved in, with its clean white planes, the park next to it like the neat green swathe around an architect's model, studded with foam trees. They could hardly believe they could afford it. Henry worked in a factory that made transistors and semiconductors; the company was on the up, buying other firms, and they were both optimistic about his prospects. The Plestor had represented a dream, a bright, modern future far away from the bomb sites and empty buildings of their childhoods. Michael was just a baby when they put their money down, another baby on the way; what they were buying into was something neither of them could have articulated, and so the disappointment that attended its failure to materialise—marked by the closure first of the nearby swimming baths, then the art deco cinema, the proliferation of pound shops and the gradual descent of the doctor's surgery into grimy disorder—had been impossible to talk about either.

Although it was the little park to which Sophia would have said she was most attached, the flat itself had become, over long years, a perfect reflection of the old lady's spirit. Despite her growing stiffness, and her hip, Sophia kept it spotlessly clean, and light flooded in for most of the day, filtering through the leaves in summer and lending the well-proportioned rooms a cool, almost underwater feel.

The parquet in the hallway was patinated to a deep shine, and in the kitchen a brown teapot, six mismatched mugs and a Cornish striped milk jug

11

gleamed on the dresser. Everything in the flat had a story to tell: some of the furniture had belonged once to Sophia's mother; some she and Henry had bought second-hand and, together, restored; he had been a practical man who hated to see good things go to waste. The sun-faded curtains and cushions she had made herself; over the years the print had passed in and out of fashion more than once, but Sophia had loved them when she made them, and she loved them now. The other flats in the block—sublet, divided into bedsits, thumping with music—may have descended into relative disorder, but Sophia's remained a haven of tranquillity. The only note of untidiness was the kitchen windowsill, where stones, pine cones, honesty seeds and dull, wizened conkers spoke of a habit that may have formed when Sophia's two children were small, but had continued long after they were grown up.

Monday morning had dawned damp and chill, and now she wiped the condensation from the inside of the kitchen window with her sleeve, the better to see if it was a stormcock singing so loudly from the top of the rowan. Its brave red berries made it one of her favourite trees in the park, especially in a breeze when its leaves would flicker to show their silvery underneaths. In truth, though, she loved all of them, and knew them all, too: which of the horse chestnuts unfurled its acid-green leaves first each spring, where the squirrels had a drey in the holm oak and whether the young cherry, its bark stripped by dogs one hot night in June, was likely to survive the coming winter, or was dying already, its sap unable to reach up past the wound.

Today's main job was to go to the post office and pay some bills. By about ten o'clock the paths that criss-crossed the grass were mainly free of charging dogs, pushchairs and other irritations; ignoring the sensible shoes her daughter Linda had bought her, Sophia Adams, seventy-eight and a half, thrust her feet into the too-big brogues she still could not bear to throw out after fourteen years of widowhood, took up her ash stick and set out.

It wasn't much of a park, really, more a strip of land between the noisy high road and the flats. The council had laid tarmac paths across it here and there, but narrow tracks of beaten earth—what the planners called 'desire paths'—had been made by feet, and better reflected where people actually wanted to go: from the estate to the bus stop, for instance, and from the benches to the pedestrian crossing.

Despite its size and situation the strip of grass was beautiful—if you had the eyes to see. The Victorians had bequeathed it an imaginative collection of trees; not just the ubiquitous planes and sycamores, and not the easy-care lollipops of cherries either, but hornbeams, service trees, acacias and Turkey oaks with bristly acorn cups like little sea anemones. It was alive with squirrels, jays and wood mice, while in spring thrushes let off football rattles from the treetops, and every few summers stag beetles emerged to rear and fence and mate, and begin another perilous generation among the logs that were left to decay here and there by governmental decree.

It was a big city, but it was a small park, and it had its own citizens and supplicants, of which Sophia supposed she was one. Today there was no sign of the little boy she often saw, the one who seemed to miss so much school, but rounding the back of the flats, ah yes, there was the Turkish chap from the fried chicken parlour having his morning cigarette on the benches.

At the other end of the park an elderly Jamaican man in tracksuit bottoms and a grubby vest was limbering up for another day's work. He spent the mornings and early evenings energetically petitioning the traffic for change and cigarettes, dancing about on the pavement as he waited for the lights to bring the cars to a halt, and sometimes in the road, too. Goodness only knows what he got up to in the afternoons; cards, perhaps. How ever does he know my name? thought Sophia whenever she found herself at the thinner end of the wedge-shaped park. It was a mystery. She always smiled and waved back at him nonetheless, poor man. Good manners cost nothing, after all.

This morning, though, Sophia headed in the opposite direction, towards the shops. A light rain had begun to fall, but she stopped under the rowan and craned her head back as far as she dared to see if she could spot whoever had been singing in it. The branches were empty of birds, but, 'Quite right, too,' she said aloud. 'I could be anyone.' She pushed her hands deep into the pockets of her coat, finding a shape that could be either a pebble or a Minto. Did she dare suck it and see? she wondered, snorting to think what her daughter would say if she caught her eating stones. 'She'd pack me off!' Sophia exclaimed, aloud. The Turkish man looked down and smiled a little to himself as the old lady passed by.

*   *   *

By mid-afternoon the drizzle had cleared, a high breeze sending the weather east where it would dampen the decking in countless suburban gardens and form shallow, dirty puddles on the sky-blue covers of backyard trampolines, most of which would remain covered up now until spring. Over the park the sky was a flat, high white, the autumn sun not quite strong enough to break through or fully dry the rain-darkened tarmac paths.

The tea tray at four was a daily ritual: on it a clean tea cloth, the deep brown teapot, the striped jug, a mug and spoon and two biscuits on a side plate. Sophia took it carefully to her kitchen table and sat down, Basildon Bond and a biro before her. She was trying to write a letter to her pen pal, who also happened to be her granddaughter, but it wasn't always easy to think of things to say to someone of only eight. They had begun the letters, despite living just round the corner from each other, after the correspondent assigned to Daisy by her school failed to reply to Daisy's email. At first their letters had been something of a novelty, but now she rather suspected that Daisy's brief and increasingly dilatory replies were composed rather under duress.

'*Dear Daisy*,' she began. While her cramped handwriting came only haltingly, in her mind the lines ran clear and true as thought.

But then, from outside her window came a sudden, clanking roar and a medley of indistinct male shouts. Sophia switched off Radio 4 and craned forward to see. It was a small yellow JCB, and it was being driven into the park followed by two men in council overalls carrying sacks. 'Goodness me,' she said, standing up. It stopped under the big plane tree, about a hundred yards away, and the men in overalls threw down their sacks, sat down on them and began to smoke. The driver reversed up a little and raised the JCB's mechanical arm, before bringing it down and tearing up the grass in a long strip. Before long it had rucked up the turf like an unmade bed, which the two workmen heaved and rolled to one side. The soil beneath was black and startling, like a wound immodestly revealed. Then the machine went to work again, piling the earth to the other side of the wide, shallow trench. Finally the driver switched off the engine. The other two men tore open the tops of the sacks and stepped down into the hole. Bulbs, she thought, picturing the local squirrels and how the smell of disturbed earth was an irresistible challenge to them. She wondered what sort of bulbs they were. Daffs, probably.

The men were rather a long time in the hole, and eventually Sophia went back to her letter. After a while she heard the JCB roar into life, and looked out of the window again. The arm was swinging down to scoop up the black earth from the pile in its claw, before letting it drop again into the hole. Then the men kicked it roughly into place before pushing and rolling the muddy turf back over the top. Once the driver had run over it with his caterpillar tracks you would hardly have known that anything had happened there.

Over the next hour or so the three-man crew repeated the procedure over near the benches and in a long, thin strip by the road. At about five, just as she was considering a walk to the shops and a look at what they had been up to, she heard the JCB's engine roar closer and closer, until she could almost make out what the men were shouting at each other over it. It drew right up to the chain-link fence, sending Sophia back from her window to the kitchen door, from where she watched as it tore up the grass and the daisies, the stubborn buttercups and next year's dandelions, revealing the naked soil beneath with its secret cargo of red worms, ants and fat white grubs.

Finally the driver backed off a few feet, switched off the engine and began to roll a cigarette. The men with the sacks stepped into the hole and began to set out the golden bulbs. Sophia craned forward to see: they were placing them in neat rows to make a grid, each one the same distance from its neighbour. How extraordinary, she thought. They must have been told to plant them six inches apart.

'Half five!' came a shout, just as she was filling the kettle for more tea. The men were kicking soil roughly over the bulbs and locking up the JCB, which crouched by the strips of torn-up turf, the ends of its tines glinting dully. By the time the kettle had boiled, they were gone. Sophia drank her tea at the kitchen table and considered the regiment of bulbs half buried beneath her window.

*   *   *

It was after midnight when she left the flat, having stayed up late through a combination of television, tea and pacing about. As she grasped her ash stick and pulled the door to behind her, she was aware of several things: that wandering about in the park at night might be considered foolhardy by some; that she was a silly and quite possibly mad old woman; and that this level of subterfuge—including the fact that she was wearing an old black coat of Henry's—was probably unnecessary. But you can't always be sensible, she thought, and anyway, some things are too important. They had both always loved the park and had taken a keen interest in its upkeep, but it was after Henry's death that she had really felt it to be her responsibility. Henry would have had something to say about the grids of bulbs, she felt. And besides, she didn't want to have to look at them like that next spring.

When she rounded the corner of her building, Sophia was relieved to find the park empty. There were no rowdy youngsters occupying the benches, no late-night dog walkers either. On the other side of the grass, cars and buses rumbled by, and some distance off in the direction of the shops a siren wailed and then cut out. The moon was out and nearly full, reefed in cloud; it wasn't raining, although the air felt damp, and for the most part the park was still.

Sophia realised she was holding her breath. She let it out with a puff and went to sit on the benches for a moment. Behind them, generations of rotting leaves and council indifference had allowed brambles and nettles to run riot, while ivy had swarmed up the chain-link fence, black and glossy-looking in the moonlight. Now the tangled thicket harboured beer cans, mice and, doubtless, rats, given the chicken bones and takeaway boxes in the bin. Michaelmas, she thought; the final day for eating blackberries. Yesterday, rather. Not that anyone did, here. It was a shame, but that meant all the more for the mice, and they were far more deserving.

Here and there among the brambles pale circles

18

shook and gleamed in the moonlight. Sophia had planted the first honesty seeds there—how many years ago? She no longer knew. Their purple flowers came up in spring, when she would come with secateurs and surreptitiously cut the bramble stems to give them a fighting chance, but it was in autumn that she loved them best, when the flowers gave way to flat, round seed pods like little moons. Now she sat down and reached carefully over the back of the bench to strip the silvery discs from the stems, and put them in her pocket.

She got up and approached the hole, which was bigger than it had looked from the kitchen. The pile of earth beside it retained the inner dimensions of the digger's claw here and there, she saw, in brief angles and surfaces. Leaning heavily on her stick, she managed to lower herself into a kneeling position. It wasn't elegant, but then so little was these days. Had she ever been elegant? she wondered. Probably not.

Some of the bulbs hadn't been covered up at all, and so were easy to spot in the faint light falling from her kitchen window on the other side of the fence. She picked one up and brushed the soil from it; its papery skin was not unlike her own. Yet underneath it wasn't pulpy, but firm and waxy, waiting to push up through the cold soil with all the coiled energy of spring. It smelled of earth and rain.

Painstakingly, Sophia fished the rest of the bulbs from their rows and piled them up on the grass beside the hole. There were fifty-seven. She could feel her knees stiffening, and knew there'd be hell to pay tomorrow. With her bare hands she scooped as much of the soil to one side as she could, feeling the good dirt working its way up under her fingernails, and every so often the cold, wet softness of a worm.

She sat on the edge of the hole for a moment, thinking through what to do next. Then, she began to fill her pockets with bulbs until Henry's greatcoat was bulging with them, as were her cardigan pockets underneath. Using her stick and the metal fence, she slowly stood up, her moon shadow faint and ghostly on the grass.

In the dark, the hole looked as deep as a grave. Sophia began to throw the bulbs in one by one, letting them land wherever they would.

Finally, the bulbs were all in the ground. Sophia cast into the pit the honesty pods, and the flat seeds which had made their way out of them into the crevices of Henry's pockets. Finally, and laboriously, she kicked the earth back in from the sides to cover the bulbs. Perhaps it didn't look exactly as it had when the men from the council had clocked off, but she was willing to bet that tomorrow morning they would simply roll back the turf and move on to the next job.

Back at home, Sophia's face was a pale blur in the black glass of her kitchen window. Before going to bed she scrubbed her old hands with Fairy and a nail brush, but it would be days before they were entirely clean again.

3

DOG WHIPPING DAY

TC typed the name in again and hit return. There were lots of hits—some of them nothing like his dad, even some from abroad. Some of them were kids on Facebook, or people who had won things or done crimes. He clicked through to the next page, and the next. There must be a way you did it—find people. Like detectives, or police. How did you do it, if you didn't even know what city to look in, if the person had been gone for months now? He didn't know.

'Do you need any help?' It was the librarian, nosying up behind him.

TC hit the 'x', slung his bag on his back and headed for maths. His dad had probably written to him or something, and she'd chucked it. There was no way he'd just have left TC behind. Her, maybe; but not him. He'd have to start checking the post, find a way to be around when it came. Or just go through the bins.

In the corridor he was careful about eye contact, timing too. It was best not to be noticed. Sometimes you got put on the spot, asked questions and there wasn't a right answer. Or there was something wrong about you, what you were wearing or doing. It wasn't bullying—that was being punched and kicked—it was just that he was weird, and it was obvious. He couldn't even blame them for noticing; he could see it himself. It leaked out of him, he couldn't help it. Like you weren't allowed

21

to say certain jokes, because it came out wrong in your voice somehow, and then you'd get called a try-hard. It was just how things were, and trying to change it only made it worse.

It had been different with his dad. With his dad he'd felt like he was popular or something; interesting. He could say stuff and his dad didn't laugh, unless he meant him to. Not that his dad was perfect or anything, not that everything had been like a film or whatever before he had gone, but he did actually like TC. Or love him or whatever.

His mum could see what the other kids thought of him, TC knew, but his dad thought everything was fine. That was good, because if he'd seen it he'd have thought it too. So it all had to be kept separate; inside. The fact that he was used to it didn't mean it was easy.

When the police brought him home that day it had been awful. That man there, in their flat. First there was the police thing to get through; they wanted to talk to his mum about him, give them both grief. 'Is this the boy's father?' they asked; he'd sworn at them then, got a talking-to.

The man—Jamal, she said his name was, like anyone cared—got lost fast. Then it was just him and his mum, looking at each other while the coppers went on about whatever. When they left, then it kicked off. He tried to imagine his dad, what he would want him to do. But he couldn't do anything, not really. He was only a kid.

He'd been back since: Jamal, his mother's . . . what? Friend? He cooked them steaks, the first TC had ever had. And when it got cold he brought TC some gloves. Jamal wanted TC to like him, and with a hard-learned sense of playground

22

ruthlessness TC knew that put him beneath regard.

'Is he your boyfriend, then?' TC asked as they watched telly one night.

'Look, TC—'

'You shouldn't have a boyfriend.'

'Well, luckily it ain't up to you.'

'What about Dad?'

'What about him?'

'Are you gonna tell him?'

'Tell him?'

'When he gets back. Because I am.'

'TC—your dad ain't coming back.'

'Yes he is.'

'He ain't, OK?'

'Why not?'

'Cos it's over.'

'You won't let him come back. He'd come back but you won't let him.'

'It ain't like that.'

'What, then?'

But she turned the telly up and told him to get off her back.

*   *   *

Maths went on for years. He was good at it, something he made sure none of the other kids knew; as long as you didn't put your hand up it was OK.

It was too cold to go to the common, so after school TC went home, climbing the four flights despite the fact that the lift, for once, was working. He hated the lift, though; it was like being eaten by the huge building, going up and down in its throat like an Adam's apple—and anyway, the stairs were easy.

His mum was asleep on the settee, the lounge stale and close, so he got some crisps and went to his room. It was big enough only for his bed with its old blue covers, and a little chest of drawers; his clothes and things mostly went in a plastic zip-up hamper under the bed. It was OK, though; it had a door he could shut, and a window, level with the tree canopy, that looked down to the waste ground behind the tower blocks. It was almost like a hide.

He got out all his Lego men from a box under the bed and made them fight with his Luke Skywalker. Even though Luke didn't have a head he was still much stronger than they were, and they couldn't beat him. TC had almost a whole shoebox of Lego. Other people took it to school sometimes to show what they'd made, but he didn't want to. What if you lost some, or someone took it? No, it was better just to keep it and play with it by yourself.

When he'd finished he put everything back in the box along with a corvid skull, a stone with a hole all the way through, a lapis-blue jay's feather and a mysterious, verdigris half-pence piece that he'd found on the common, and pushed the box back under the bed.

That evening the wind shifted direction and began to blow from the north-east. It battered the tower blocks, throwing rain like gravel against the glass only to quieten, take breath, and hurl itself again. TC lay on his bed and felt the windows tremble, and pretended he was out at sea.

*   *   *

Across the high road from the block where TC lived was a dilapidated Edwardian terrace, shops below, flats above. Over the corner premises, a second-hand furniture shop now for many years, the dim shape of a man moved at a grimy sash window. The room behind him had grown dark while Jozef was working, but he whittled mostly by feel anyway.

A man's voice called his name up the bare stairwell with its stark bulb, the two syllables bouncing flatly off the walls. He stood and stretched his big hands, clicked the knuckles. 'Yes, I am coming,' he called. The rain had slowed, the wind was dropping, and the sky was pressed velvet blue against the window. Time for work.

Before leaving his little room, spartan as a monk's cell, he placed a half-finished carving no bigger than his thumb on the windowsill with its fellows. It was unclear to him what it would become, but it already had the rough lineaments of an animal. He would wait to finish it until its nature declared itself beneath his blunt fingers.

Barely an hour between the end of one job and the start of the next, and nearly all of it spent whittling. Jozef sighed to himself as he jogged down the narrow stairs to where Musa the little Turk waited for him in the darkened shop, his outline barely visible among the stacks of second-hand furniture, lamps and old TVs. The street lights flickered on as he pulled the shop door to behind them, bathing the wooden creatures on the windowsill above in flat, orange light.

It was past three when he returned, bringing with him the smell of hot fat from the takeaway in his hair and skin. A familiar whimpering attended his progress up the stairs. He did not like the dog,

25

yet he would walk it most nights rather than hear it cry in the empty upstairs room until dawn. It was ugly, bullish and simple, with a scarred muzzle and torn ears, bandy legs and a perpetual grin. It didn't have a name, so Jozef called it Znajda, but only to himself.

As he opened the door it shouldered its way out and clattered down the stairs to wait for him in the hall. There was no lead, or collar for that matter, but it never strayed more than a few paces from him, his soft whistle enough to call it instantly to his side.

Back outside, Jozef turned off the high road, away from the lurid chicken parlours, the busy night buses and the 3 a.m. altercations, and felt the first rumour of rain on his face. By the time he reached the wide open acres of the common the weather had set in, and he wished he had made for somewhere with more shelter. The dog didn't care, nosing the drifts of wet leaves a few paces ahead or falling behind for a moment to give something its particular attention, but Jozef had little love for the place and wished briefly for bed, the dip in the old grey mattress first formed by other bodies than his, but comforting enough at this time of night.

Now he took the wide path onto the common under an avenue of plane trees, which, unlike the bare horse chestnuts, still afforded a little shelter. Behind him he could hear the occasional car wash past, nearly all of them minicabs at this hour, but the particular silence of a city park was closing about him and was all the more absolute for being surrounded by such distant sounds. A siren corkscrewed up, a borough away, one of only a few that would sound for the rest of that wet night.

26

For as the weather front swept west across the city, driving its inhabitants indoors, the phones rang less frequently at the control room and more cars remained parked up idle at the police stations, the hard rain flensing the grime from their metal flanks.

Jozef and Znajda were not alone on the common. Above them roosted a silent convocation of starlings, their bodies dark balls against the greater darkness of the sky. Now and then one would shake the rain from its feathers, and a few eyed the progress of the bull terrier on the path below before settling back to sleep.

As he felt the first cold dampness enter his trainers, Jozef put his head down and picked up his pace. It was no night to be out, and he took the most direct route off the common, turning into Leasow Road, a wide, gently curving street double-parked with cars and lined with Edwardian villas, their position determined generations ago by a long-forgotten stream. Few who lived there had any idea that it still ran deep below their cellars, tamed, these days, by purposeful Victorian brickwork.

Jozef walked in and out of pools of orange light, and apart from the patter of the rain his footfalls were the only sound. The houses he passed were shut up fast against the dark, the dogs in their beds, the upstairs bedrooms thick with sleeping breath where couples spooned or slept turned away, the digital alarm clocks flicking forward unseen, the bedtime reads splayed or bookmarked neatly on the tables. Wet through and a world away, Znajda paused and shook herself before trotting stoically on.

27

*   *   *

That night, Jozef dreamed about a field on the flank of a hill whose shape he had known all his life. It was waist-high in golden grass, the gentle rise of it abuzz with crickets and bees and stroked down silver by the breeze, when it came. Then he saw that it was full of hares, racing and kicking like overwound clocks. He was holding one against his chest, and the strength in its back legs and the speed of its heart were shocking under his hands. Then it was running away from him through the tall, late-summer grass, racing left and uphill to where the dark shape of the beech hanger waited on the skyline; and though Jozef ran and ran, the dear, familiar field would come no closer, and he could not keep up.

4

HALLANTIDE

Across the country the leaves were going out in a blaze of orange and red. From Somerset to East Yorkshire the winter wheat had all been sown, and further north and west the dairy herds had been taken indoors for the winter. On Dartmoor the bracken was dying back to reveal the peat skin and granite bones of the moor beneath. Sheep farmers were busy putting their ewes to the tup, and around the field margins roared tractors with their cutter-bars extended to the side, pheasants spinning

28

and squawking before them and the hedges left square and brutal behind.

In the city the back gardens were preparing for their long hibernation. The grass's growth had slowed to a stop, and summer bedding stood sad and tangled in the pots. On sunny days the few remaining blooms seemed even lonelier, as though it was still summer and the lush beds and borders had suddenly gone over, all together, and too soon.

Jozef woke early, Denny's brisk double knock on his door reminding him they had a house clearance booked in. Downstairs, the shop, cluttered with who knew how many people's possessions, stank even more than usual of damp. Musa was sitting idle on a grubby cream sofa, thumbing his mobile phone; he often minded the shop while they were out on a job.

Denny dragged a chipboard coffee table outside to the pavement while Jozef carried out a fake leather office chair. He found the day had dawned clear and bright, the air washed lucent by the rain and his shadow crisp beneath his feet. He lit a cigarette, and together the two men carried out a sideboard with chipped veneer and a missing handle, six stacking chairs and an old pine kitchen table in two parts: first the trestle, and then the board. Smaller, more thievable items like lamps, mirrors and magazine racks remained inside the shop, as did anything upholstered until all threat of rain had passed. Wet sofas stank, and would not sell.

The clearance was only a mile or so away. Denny drove and Jozef rode shotgun, looking out at the autumn streets and thinking about home. They pulled up on the way, Denny returning to the

29

shabby van with a bacon and egg McMuffin and a sugar doughnut, but Jozef did not want to eat.

The building they arrived at had once been a grocer's, and little had been done to adapt it for use as a home. The green front door had clearly not been used for years; it gave straight into a large room fronted by two deep plate-glass windows, once the shop floor. The lower parts of the windows were papered over with yellowing newspaper, but the room inside was visible from the street around their peeling edges. It was almost empty, bar some sun-bleached leaflets and junk mail like a tide around the edges.

Now, access to the house was via a side door into the kitchen. A little room at the back was clearly where the old man had lived and died, his armchair watched over by a faded picture of the Sacred Heart. Jozef crossed himself quickly as he entered. It was dark and close, like a den, and despite being full of the dead man's last and pitiful effects there was clearly nothing there that they could sell. Jozef did not linger.

The house's contents betrayed the course of the old man's slow decline into immobility and death. Upstairs the furniture and knick-knacks dated back to the 1950s and displayed a distinctly feminine influence. A tidy downstairs parlour had clearly been occupied for much longer, and from the curling yellow copies of *Radio Times* Jozef guessed it had been in use until around the turn of the century. But finally the man had confined himself to the little back room, the galley kitchen and the lean-to lavatory, the detritus of his life hardening around him like the concentric rings left by the slow evaporation of a puddle.

Denny was upstairs with a clipboard looking over the furniture. 'We'll take the big brass bed and the wardrobe,' he called out, hearing Jozef's tread on the stairs, 'and the bedroom mirror and the dressing table from in there, and anything else catches your eye. Bathroom: nothing. Second bedroom I'm just looking at. What a fucking tip it is. Hardly worth the journey.'

The bed had already been stripped, which Jozef was glad of. The room was dim, and he pulled back the curtains from the flyblown glass. Ivy had scaled the exterior wall and was making a bid for the inside, its brute tendrils breaching the sash and hauling themselves in across the sill on clusters of tiny grey feet. The curtains drawn, the clear morning sunshine poured in, perhaps for the first time in over a decade, and revealed the waxy vigour of each leaf. Jozef thought about his dream, and about how quick nature is to reclaim what we no longer use. And he thought about his life here, how little, now, he had to leave. A few changes of clothes. Some books. The carvings.

He found the chess set in a little box on top of the wardrobe. Half the pieces were a rich red wood, the rest pale. All were smooth from having been handled through countless games over countless years. They were crudely made, of a basic design familiar to Jozef from childhood: the knights without eyes, the pawns simply stubs of turned wood. Denny did not want it for the shop, and so Jozef took it. There were no relatives to consider.

It was mid-afternoon when they finished. They left by the back door with a last load for the skip, closing the door on the pillaged house. School was over and the street outside was raucous with the

31

newly released exuberance of children. A crow hunched high on the chimney pot was joined by another as the van pulled away.

*   *   *

Denny sang along to the radio all the way back in a flat, nasal tone. At the shop, Musa helped unload the van; then, shrugging on his denim jacket and preparing to leave, he announced, 'Dog's gone.'

'What d'you mean, gone?' asked Denny.

'Is gone,' replied Musa. 'It was down here, in shop; then—gone. I look for it, but nothing.'

Denny was motionless. 'When?'

'I don't know. Two, three hours? I just think I should tell you, OK? Now I must go. I am not enough at home with my family these days. Eh, Joe, I see you later. See you tomorrow, Denny.' And he was gone.

The light was already leaching out of the autumn sky. Jozef looked at Denny, who remained staring at the shop door. 'You want I look for her?' he asked.

'Look for the dog? No, mate,' replied Denny. 'It'll come back when it's hungry. It knows what's good for it.' And with that, the subject was closed.

*   *   *

That night, returning from his evening shift at the fried-chicken takeaway, Jozef found himself wondering whether Znajda had come back. The silence on the stairs was his answer.

Earlier he had taken out the chess pieces and lined them up on the windowsill next to his

32

carvings; now he looked at them again. Thirty-two pieces. It would take him a few months to make that many, but he would enjoy the work. The only question was whether the creatures he had already made could be adapted, made to fit, or whether he should start from scratch. A rabbit, a fox, a marmot, a boar: they were animals that spoke to him of home. He recalled his dream, and it came to him that a hare would be the next animal he would make. Then he picked up the half-finished one and ran his thumb over it. Nothing, yet; but sometimes you had to give them time.

He had known, at some level, that he would have to go out and look for Znajda. He took his usual route across the common, pausing and whistling softly for her every hundred yards or so; but she didn't come. The night was dry, so rather than turn for home he quartered the little park that sat between the high road and the Plestor Estate. With several bus stops along its length it was rarely deserted, even at night, and he felt foolish whistling for a dog that didn't come, so he sat on a decaying log under the dark trees and rolled a cigarette, his big fingers deft in the dark. He could see Musa leaning on the counter in the brightly lit takeaway across the road, chewing gum, no doubt, and waiting for customers.

The dog would have come if she had heard him, he was sure of it.

5

MARTINMAS

In summer—in spring, even—it is impossible to believe in November. Snow you can picture, picture-postcard style, but the sodden, rotting tangle where the brazen nettles were, the once-secret nests now stark in the bare branches and above all the sheer dead silence of the sky—these things are unimaginable for the rest of the year.

That year, November shut the living city down without reprieve. Within a week only a few yellow leaves remained on the trees on the common, fluttering like prayer flags against the leaden sky.

TC loved this time of year. Like most children, he was on intimate terms with the earth. The under-tens deal in little sticks and pebbles; they are artisans of holes, experts in the types and properties of stones; they appreciate the many qualities of mud and its summer corollary, dust. And then they grow up, and the ground is just whatever's underfoot.

What TC most liked about the ground in winter were the clues it gave up about everything that went on that was secret. For instance, toads hibernated under the abandoned paving stones at the end of the communal gardens behind his block of flats. They left slick, fat-bodied runnels where they pushed themselves through the chill mud; and if he heaved up a slab, there they'd be, loath and cold and liable to release a bitter flood if picked up, as though his careful hands were a heron's beak, or an otter's jaws. And one evening, after the bins had been plundered again, he had taken a twig and swept the earth smooth near the flats' refuse area, and sprinkled a fine tilth over it; the very next morning it bore the neat, precise pad marks of a fox.

*　　　*　　　*

On the night of the tenth the skies slowly cleared, and for the first time that year the frost penetrated the heart of the city, and cities nationwide. In the morning TC woke early and looked down at the white rime on the grass and the crazed panes on the puddles concealing the icy liquid mud beneath. Already he could see that there were actual animal tracks crossing the yard below.

It was gloves weather, but the only pair he had were the ones his mother's boyfriend, Jamal, had got for him, and he didn't want to wear them. In the past, when he had been given something new, he had always tucked it in with his other things for a night so that they could tell it all about what kind of boy he was, but this time TC had simply left the gloves on his bedroom floor. However, bursting out of the back door into the dazzling winter sun, unwashed and unbreakfasted, it was only a moment before he dived back in, retrieved the gloves and re-emerged, snapping the plastic thread that joined them together and pulling them on. Some things were too important.

For the most part, birds were too light to leave footprints in the frost, though TC could see a magpie leaving a trail near the back of the yard as its long tail brushed the ground behind it. What

35

he was more interested in was the larger track that traversed the yard in a bold, straight line, starting by the bins on the right and leading across the frosted grass to the hedge on the left where a gap led into the overgrown area behind the neighbouring block of flats.

He examined what he could of the trail, careful to keep his own footprints clear. It was likely to have been left by a fox, he knew, but that didn't make it any less interesting. What had it been up to? And where had it gone? Perhaps he could follow the prints to its den. Here and there the ground, still muddy beneath the covering of frost, bore the clear impression of a paw, and suddenly TC's heart was in his mouth as he saw the size of the pads. Whatever had been in his garden was too big for a fox, and far too heavy.

The tracks were like a fox's, but bigger, and badgers didn't live in the city, he knew that. He knew that none of the prints in the book looked right. The tracks must have been left by something unusual.

He felt a shiver of excitement at the thought that something lonely and wild lived somewhere near him, something that nobody else knew about. Perhaps he could make friends with it. No, he knew that wasn't possible. But perhaps it would come to know that he didn't mean it any harm. He could put food out, if only he could be sure what it was and what it would want to eat. It would learn to trust him, after a while. No one else would be able to go near it; it would only allow him and nobody else, not even police or zookeepers. It would be the two of them, out there together in the forgotten, wild corners of the city, and perhaps one day he would rescue it from something. Or it would rescue him.

TC knew he did not have long before the sun began to burn off the frost. Ducking low, he pushed himself through the hedge into the shadows beneath next door's yew. He had played there many times before, and for a while had kept things in a crevice in the trunk, but this time the familiar place was transformed as he felt the thrill of following so exactly in a wild creature's footsteps.

The yew was three hundred years old and kept the ground beneath it barren and dry, and useless for tracking. He began to look for clues in the surrounding undergrowth to tell him which way the animal had gone, but it was choked thick with ground elder and brambles, and despite his utter and total concentration he could see nothing.

*   *   *

Jamal laughed when he looked down from the bedroom window and saw TC creeping around in next door's yard. The boy was strange, all right, but he was pleased to see him wearing the gloves he had bought.

He cranked open the window, letting the chill November air drive out the stale smoke inside.

'Come inside, kid,' he called down. 'You'll catch your death. It's Saturday, anyway. I'm gonna make eggs for you and your mother.'

Jamal worked in the kitchen of a hotel in town, and his cooking was something else. Once he had made them all pizzas from scratch, even the dough, something TC would not have considered possible until he had seen it done.

Now TC raced in, climbing the stairs in record

37

time, but once at the kitchen table found he did not know what to say. It was perhaps the first time he had been alone with his mother's boyfriend, although he had been visiting the flat for a few weeks now.

Jamal regarded him for a moment, then turned back to the stove and rattled a pan of muffins under the grill. 'What you doing out there, anyway?' he asked, more gruffly than he had meant. TC looked down at his hands. He took the gloves off and stuffed them in his pockets.

'Eh? TC?' Jamal tried, more gently. 'Yous always out there, huntin' around. Looks like you got some exciting stuff going on. I'm curious, thas all.'

'Nothing,' said TC. 'Just looking at stuff.'

'What stuff?'

'Just . . . birds and stuff.'

'What, you a birdwatcher, TC? For real?' Jamal whistled through his teeth. 'Well, well. What do they do then, your birds? Cos when I see 'em, they just walk about and shit on stuff.'

TC was caught between the urge to tell Jamal to fuck off and inform him that there was a dangerous animal living in the garden. Unable to do either, he stood, his face congested.

'What?' said Jamal, turning round from the stove. But it was too late. The boy was already clattering down the stairwell, the flat door banging shut behind him.

The muffins began to send out gentle curls of smoke as Jamal bent to pick up the boy's gloves from the cracked lino. He pushed one inside the other to make a neat ball, and placed it thoughtfully on the kitchen table.

TC crossed the road to cut through the little

38

park, and walked down Leasow Road to the common. The bark of the lone ash tree near the children's play area was wet and black, the branches jutting obscenely smooth from the tumorous bole, their grey fingers beckoning. TC touched it once, for luck, and thought about wolves.

*   *   *

At Sophia's daughter's house on Leasow Road Saturday mornings meant a leisurely breakfast and sport on the radio. Linda was not yet back from Friday's conference, held at a smart hotel in Chichester, and a faint but unmistakable atmosphere of misrule hung about the house. Daisy had come downstairs in her pyjamas and her father had made them both porridge, and they had maple syrup with it, eating together at the kitchen table as Steven read the paper and Daisy hummed to herself and looked at the things that fell out of it.

'Daddy, can we have chickens?' she asked, brandishing a leaflet at him over the top of the paper. 'Look! And then we would get our eggs for free!'

'No, love, they'd ruin the garden,' replied Steven, deep in Finance.

'No they wouldn't, they live in the little pink house, see? Or blue, if you wanted. Or green.'

'And they smell.'

'No they don't, Daddy, chickens don't smell. They're birds. Birds don't smell,' and she giggled to think of it.

'And they make too much noise, and a fox might eat them.'

'It wouldn't, Daddy! They live in the little house!'

39

But she only half meant it. A kitten was what she actually wanted, and she wouldn't be able to have a cat if they had chickens. She picked up the next leaflet, and began to read out loud about a range of French-style iron cookware instead.

After breakfast Daisy stayed in her pyjamas for quite a long time, just to see what happened. It turned out nothing did, so she got dressed, putting all her worst things on together.

'What shall we do today, Daddy, make cupcakes?' she asked hopefully. She liked the mixing bit best, and also the tasting bit, at which she was very good.

Steven was in the study looking at the computer; Daisy fidgeted in the doorway, something about her right foot suggesting that having a gentle kick at the door frame would not be impossible. 'I do know how, it's easy.'

'Don't kick the door frame, love,' said Steven. He hadn't even noticed her clothes.

'Or shall we go out on our bikes?'

'Have you done all your homework?'

'*Ye-e-e-es*,' Daisy replied, drawing out the word. His eyes still on the screen, Steven put out one arm, and so she climbed onto his lap and faced the computer. Sometimes he would be making exciting 3D models of things that didn't yet exist because that was his job, but this time he was writing boring emails.

'Give me five minutes, love. Then we're going to pop to the bottle bank, and then how would you like to go and see your gran?'

'Yay!' Daisy cheered and wriggled off his lap. 'I have to finish my letter first, then.' And she ran upstairs.

40

Linda was heading home on the centre lane of the motorway at a steady seventy, a headache threatening but held at bay with painkillers. The conference had gone well, so far as she could tell. No major disasters; not logistically, anyway. A couple of people had drunk too much, as usually happened, but office politics weren't her problem.

Linda was an events organiser. She counted several big firms among her clients, all of which had offices in several cities. Consequently she drove nearly every day, either to see clients or suppliers, or to visit the hotels and conference centres she used for their departmental jollies, quarterly meetings and team-building exercises.

The hours spent on the road made her car something of a second home. She loved the feeling of freedom it gave her, the sense of being in total control of the little microcosm of her immediate environment: the climate, the soundtrack, the speed, the direction. She even liked the smell of it: warm plastic, air-freshener, upholstery. There was nothing in the car she couldn't control, and nothing outside it she couldn't shut out or escape from. In it she was answerable to nobody, inviolable.

Sometimes she would imagine her journeys criss-crossing a map of the British Isles, like the one her father had pinned to the wall of the flat when she and Michael were small. There were few cities, or even large towns, she hadn't driven to now. She imagined thumbtacks on the map, threads wound between them like a web. She had covered the whole country over the years, and the routes were all filed away in her head, intersection by intersection. Nobody could say she didn't know the territory.

She often wondered what her father would have made of her job. 'Organising parties?' Sophia had said when she'd first started. 'My word, you'd think they could do something as easy as that for themselves, wouldn't you?' She hadn't meant anything by it, Linda knew, but at the same time a simple 'Well done, love' would have meant a lot. Her mother had never been like that, though: demonstrative. Not that she hadn't been pleased with Linda when she did well at school, for instance, but it had never seemed to be enough. She had tried to talk to Michael about it one Christmas, years ago, but he had just laughed, told her she was being oversensitive. It hadn't mattered so much when they'd both been alive, but now, when she visited the flat she grew up in, she couldn't help noticing the things her mother didn't say that her father would have. It was as though part of her blamed her mother for not standing in for him now that he was gone, for not *being him*.

And since her father's death there had been more to it, too, a hard grain of resentment at how little her mother had seemed to grieve. It was as though she had simply picked up the threads of her life and carried on, and if she mourned she gave no real sign of it to Linda. But why should she, Steven had put to her gingerly. Grief was not some kind of debt; her mother didn't owe her daughter her tears.

Yet in the days following Henry's death they had both assumed that Sophia would fall apart; she and Steven had been ready to take her in, had braced themselves for months of dependency, years even.

And they had been glad, then—hadn't they?—to see that she would cope by herself after all.

In the fourteen years since Henry died Sophia had stubbornly refused to leave the estate, despite its growing squalor. They had even offered to find her a little garden flat nearby—at considerable expense—but the old woman wouldn't budge, and Linda simply could not understand why. After all, it might have been smart once, but now the upstairs balconies were cluttered with bikes and dead plants and satellite dishes, and it was so removed from the place of her childhood memories as to be, in her mind, almost a different place. These days the Plestor was yet another part of the city she tried to blank out, like the awful high road, the tower blocks and the terraced row of squats near the station.

Linda sighed and checked the satnav: nearly an hour to go. Every couple of hundred yards, it seemed, the motorway exhorted her: check your distance, take a break, keep two chevrons apart. She passed signs for villages and towns she could barely believe in. Cars turned off to go to them, their drivers taking their familiar turnings home; people spending their whole lives in places she had never even heard of.

Except for the odd pine plantation, or stand of silver birches with their dazzling white trunks and fuzz of plum-coloured branches, the thickets that flashed past were low and uniformly dun. From the car it was impossible to say what kind of trees they were.

Once, her journey would have taken several days, and would have required an intimacy with the lineaments of the landscape that is now almost unimaginable. It could have taken many routes,

43

rather than the few today prescribed by roads, and would have negotiated hills, plains, forests and escarpments which were now little more than antique words on a map—and which did not even appear on the A3-sized road atlas tucked into the pocket behind the passenger seat of Linda's car, nor on the satnav suckered to the screen. The journey Linda made was mostly formed from letters and numbers, and the waymarks weren't rivers or even towns but service stations, with their liminal populations and wagtail-haunted car parks, and interchanges that looked like Scalextric tracks on her GPS.

Yet although all she saw of the shape and texture of the country she lived in was what was visible in a varying strip either side of the road, it was still there, unseen yet unchanged in its essentials for centuries: the ancient contours of the land over which the cars now crawled in inconsequential lines, contours which would persist long after the roads had gone. The hamlets and tiny churches, founded for good reason on bluffs or by streams, endured despite the motorway which now scythed past and left them unmoored, while under the tarmac slept the detritus of a thousand lives: coins and bones, belt buckles and curses, things that had been lost and things that had been thrown away.

*　　　*　　　*

Daisy was bored of writing her letter. She wanted to play in the garden, but the gardener was there and she wasn't supposed to disturb him. She went to her playroom to look at her toys, instead; she had a toy cupboard and a wooden chest, both stuffed with fashion dolls, computer games and boxes of things she hadn't even opened. Each birthday more came, especially if she had a proper birthday party, and although her mum gave some to the poor children there were still loads left. They were mostly pink, and they were all boring. Boys got all the best toys, everybody knew.

'Come on, love,' Steven called up the stairs, 'bottle bank.'

'In a second!' Daisy shouted back. 'Nearly finished.'

'I want to play in the garden but I can't because the man is here doing cutting and tidying,' she wrote. *'Your park is much nicer. If I run away one day I will come and live in it. You can play in it with me but only when I say. Now I am going to the bottle bank, which is fun. Goodbye. Love from Daisy.'* And she ran downstairs to where Steven waited with a box of wine bottles for the big hopper at the end of the road. The council took glass in the weekly recycling, but Daisy loved to push the bottles into the hoppers' rubber mouths and hear them crash satisfyingly inside.

It was only a few minutes further to Sophia's flat. Unlike his wife, Steven had no problem visiting the Plestor Estate. He couldn't understand why she behaved as though the place was some kind of ghetto, when it was only just round the corner from Leasow Road's sought-after properties. Cities could be like that, of course; different areas, different people, all butting up against each other. But he felt that it was good for Daisy to spend time there. Her private school was like a little hothouse, and most of her time off was managed or educational in some way.

When they had first got married they had lived on the other side of the city—almost as far from the estate as it was possible to get. Then, when they were trying for a baby, they decided to move, and the pull of family, an area they knew and a good school, had led them back. Neither of them had meant to end up quite so close to Sophia, yet there were things in life you chose without meaning to, and sometimes—although his wife would never admit it—sometimes the world you grew up in turned out to be stronger than you could predict.

'I'll pick you up at about five,' he said, kissing Daisy goodbye at the entrance to the estate and waving to Sophia where she looked out from her kitchen window.

'I saw a hedgehog!' shouted Daisy by way of greeting, as she barrelled into the flat and began kicking off her shoes.

'Hello, Daisy. Did you now? How exciting,' replied Sophia. 'What was he up to?'

'I don't know because I didn't actually see him, but I think he was eating slugs,' Daisy replied. 'I heard him, and Mummy heard him. He made a snuffling noise.'

'Goodness,' said Sophia, wondering to herself that there were any slugs left in Linda's tidy garden. 'I expect he'll want to hibernate soon.'

'Yes, and he'll probably do it in our garden, I think,' said Daisy.

'Let's hope so,' said Sophia, trying to think whether there was anywhere untidy or undisturbed enough for a small mammal to sleep safely for several months. 'Now, today we have a very important job to do, and I especially need your help.'

46

'Is it outside? Can we have a picnic while we're doing it?'

'I think it's probably too chilly for that, sweet pea—but you're right, we are going to need to keep our strength up. Let's make a packed lunch to take with us.'

Daisy's eyes grew round. 'Can I have a fizzy drink?'

'No, but you can have chocolate spread. In fact, I can too,' said Sophia, assembling a sliced loaf, Nutella and tinfoil on the kitchen table.

*   *   *

Outside in the little park Daisy carried the sandwiches in her backpack, while Sophia took charge of the notebook and pen. They were counting how many dreys the squirrels were building for winter, and they began at the far end where there was a row of plane trees. Now that the leaves were coming down it was possible to see the dreys quite clearly, although left to her own devices Daisy would have recorded every magpie's nest and trapped plastic bag too.

They ate their sandwiches on the benches, Sophia letting Daisy drink apple juice out of Henry's old hip flask and both of them pretending it was whisky.

Sophia didn't spot the boy straight away. He had slipped in near the children's play area and was crouching beneath the holm oak when she saw him, looking at something on the ground. It was the lonely little lad who wagged school, she realised; and it occurred to her that, at one time, local children used to play with each other.

47

'Right, miss,' she said to Daisy, 'now for the difficult part. We have to write up all our data—that's everything we've learned—very carefully in this notebook. It could take an awfully long time.'

Daisy looked past her, brow furrowing. 'OK,' she said, without enthusiasm. 'But, Granny, you've got the best writing, so you could do all the writing and I could just help you.'

'Well, I think it would be best if we did it together,' said Sophia, 'unless . . . I don't suppose you'd prefer to go and say hello to that little boy over there, would you? He looks like he might be doing a project that needs some expert help.'

'Oh, OK then,' said Daisy, 'I'll do that instead. If you can definitely manage by yourself.'

'I'll be quite all right,' said Sophia, settling back on the bench and feeling in her pocket for a Minto. It was a shame there was only apple juice in the hip flask, but you couldn't have everything.

TC was still squatting and examining the ground when Daisy ran over. 'What are you looking at?' she demanded.

He seemed to shrink a little. 'Nothing,' he muttered.

'No it isn't. What is it? I'm Daisy. What's your name?'

'TC,' he muttered.

'TC? That's not a name,' replied Daisy. 'But you can be called it if you want. I'm eight. How old are you?'

'Nine,' said TC.

'Nine!' breathed Daisy, clearly impressed. 'Have you found something? Is it a secret?'

TC looked up, but there was no mockery in her face. He didn't want to tell; at least, he didn't think he did. But he could feel that he was going to. Why?

'You can't tell anyone,' he said.

'Cross my heart and hope to die,' the girl said, crouching down too.

'It's not a game.'

'I promise.'

TC took a deep breath. 'It's an animal.'

'What is?'

'It lives around here.'

'In the park?'

'And on the common. You know.'

'How do you know?'

'I've been tracking it.'

'What does that mean?'

'Following it. Its footprints and things.'

Daisy looked down at the ground between them. It was bare where the grass gave out beneath the holm oak's shade. 'Is there a footprint here?'

'Not yet,' replied TC, smoothing the dusty surface of the soil with his hand, 'but there might be tomorrow.'

When Sophia opened her eyes she saw that the two children were happily engrossed in whatever they had found under the tree. She hoped Daisy wasn't being too imperious with the little boy; he could clearly do with gentle handling.

But TC didn't mind Daisy's bossiness, had hardly noticed it, in fact. Although he hadn't exactly been keeping track, the truth was it was the first friendly contact he had had with another child in nearly a year.

*   *   *

49

Over the weekend it became clear to Jamal that TC was not birdwatching. He saw the boy crawling about in the undergrowth at the end of the flats' gardens, looking everywhere but at the pigeons and crows and what-all that Jamal could see in the trees. He asked Kelly about it on Sunday night as they watched TV.

'He's trying to find animals,' she said, cracking open a beer. 'You know, footprints and stuff. He's got a book on it.'

'TC got a book?' asked Jamal. 'How come we don't see him reading it?'

'I told you, it's a secret. He thinks I don't know. He's got a ghost one too.'

'But why? Why are they a secret?'

'I don't know. It's just . . . kids, yeah? You know, they like to have secret games. Keeps him quiet, anyway.'

'Can't be much for him to find,' said Jamal. 'Apart from rats.'

'He used to go on walks with his dad, though, stuff like that. He was good with him.'

'He hit you, you said.'

'Yeah. But he never laid a hand on the kid. TC still thinks his dad's perfect.'

'Well, tell him then.'

'Don't be stupid, Jamal. Why would I do that? Anyway, he would've learned it soon enough.'

'What do you mean?'

'He would've pissed Lenny off sooner or later, challenged him. Then it would've started. That fucking man, you know? The kid's got no idea. You think he's having a hard time now? You don't know how hard it would've got for him. He thinks I don't care, but he don't know what I saved him from.'

50

She loved the boy, of course she did, but she had had to put the feeling away somewhere, and now it was hard to find. She'd thought it might get easier with Lenny gone, but TC was so much like his father, and he wore the pain of missing him like a badge, held it out mutely to her, when it was as much as she could do to get herself back together. And he didn't even know the full story, he had no right to judge. Christ, she was only twenty-eight. She was allowed a life, wasn't she?

Now and then she would go into his room at night and look at him as he slept, and then she would find her feelings for him clear and uncomplicated again. It was just that life—how hard it had become, and how bleak—always got in the way. Somehow, her son was easier to love when he was asleep.

Her vision momentarily blurred, and she lit another cigarette off the back of the last. The dim room floated, flickering with TV light, four floors and forty-two feet up in the night sky.

6

MIDWINTER

Denny had not mentioned the dog again, and Jozef knew better than to ask. Without her to walk after his evening shifts at the takeaway he got to bed earlier, but slept badly. He found himself picturing the night-time common, the wind stripping the last leaves from the trees, the thickets inky and black. He did no whittling, and the unfinished animal on the sill reproached him for it.

On his day off Jozef took his wages to the bookies'. His luck wasn't in. It rarely was, but this time the size of his loss sickened him. He did not know why he did it, except that it allowed him to pass the time in some kind of company, although not in conversation.

The grass in the little park was beaten down, defeated, thick with mud on each side of the paths, and the little rowan was hung with icy silver drops. The last of the fallen leaves lay blackening in the gutters, and by half past four each afternoon it was dark. Leaving the bookies', Jozef whistled for Znajda as he cut across the common, but he knew she wasn't there.

Where the path drew close to the railway tracks he paused; a train was waiting for the signals to change and he could see through the desiccated stands of rosebay willowherb and nettles that bordered the chain-link fence to its yellow-lit interior, packed with commuters. A woman sat reading, thirty or so, he guessed, her dark hair tucked behind her ears and her brow furrowed in concentration. He willed her to look out to where he stood just fifteen feet or so away, the wind wild in the branches around him; but when she did he could tell that all she saw was her own reflection in the glass. The train shunted on.

The cafe had a sign that said 'Polski Sklep'. It served the things he remembered from home: cabbage rolls, *pierogi*, potatoes with *koperek*, sour milk. They let him while away the afternoons playing chess and reading the papers, and when it got dark they brought him cherry vodka, or sometimes *krupnik*, a sweet liqueur his sister used to distil at home.

Jozef tried not to let himself think about the farm any more, but it was always with him, every ditch, every stump, every field drain, every hollow. Nearly three years on, the sense of having been torn away from it still had the power to make him gasp, while the thought of it being farmed by other hands than his was like watching another man lay hands on his lover.

Its eighteen acres had been enough to support a small dairy herd and grow a little barley, using the old ways. They milked the cows in the shed— by hand when Jozef was a boy—and his mother made butter, and they sold what they produced to the government, although like everyone else his father kept some back and sold it quietly to their neighbours, or traded it for seeds or flour. They heard rumours of food shortages in the cities, and there were many things—for instance, sugar— for which they had to queue, but his mother grew vegetables and they kept a pig for bacon, and they usually had enough to eat.

Jozef was the middle child of five: two sisters preceded him, and two more came after. For him, the farm was everything: it was his future, and working on it every day with his father was a difficult but rewarding apprenticeship. By the age of twelve he could drive the jeep, trap rats, chop wood and plough a field, walking behind their gentle draught horse Aniołek and guiding the single-furrow plough through the soil. He would not have said that he loved the farm; his feelings about it were far less sentimental. It was only in exile from it that he understood how deeply implicated in its acres he had become.

He left school as soon as he could, at fifteen; his mother wanted him to go on to agricultural college, but he was needed on the farm; and besides, he thought he could learn everything he would ever need to know from his father. During the day they worked, and in the evenings he would sit by the lamp and read their battered old veterinary manual or monographs on such things as lameness and hoof care. His father would listen to the radio and carve figures from linden wood: madonnas, pietàs and St Nicholases, mostly, but sometimes smiling peasant couples and little children.

But then, when he was twenty-two, his father died. It was spring, but a sudden cold snap had iced the fields with rime and killed his mother's cabbages in the ground; he could remember passing Stefan Gruszka's orchard as he took the ancient jeep into the village and thinking that he would get no cider apples that year.

The jeep, US-built, sold to Russia and abandoned in Poland with thousands of others after the war, was precious. As the only vehicle on the farm it had to do duty as tractor, and it was battered and patched and bodged far beyond its natural life. For the last week or so, though, the clutch had been slipping. He took it to see Karol Wieczorek; years ago Karol had made himself a kind of tractor from a motorbike and parts of a trailer, and his skill with anything mechanical was unsurpassed. He waited while Karol did the work, and gave him a bottle of his sister's *krupnik* in thanks.

On his way back to the farm Jozef found the herd blocking the road, the animals agitated and jostling in the narrow space, his father nowhere in sight. Their warm breath steamed and hung above

54

them in a cloud.

He left the jeep idling and climbed up the hedge bank, craned, called his father's name. There was nothing. Then, pushing his way in sudden dread among the beasts, he found the body, as he had known he would, battered and despoiled.

He drove back to the farm with his father slumped beside him, held in place absurdly, tenderly, with rope tied like a safety belt around the seat. He could still remember the terrible sound his mother made when he laid the body on the kitchen table and went back out to bring in the herd.

Everything on the farm changed on that day, but within months the whole country had changed. Jozef remembered the euphoria of the election well, and the sadness that Poland was moving forward so fast without his father. But there was little time to mourn; with the fall of Communism farmers like him had to scramble to find a way to sell their produce. The village was suddenly full of men trying to sell their milk, and at first the price dropped below even what the government had paid; but it wasn't long before new companies had sprung up, their milk tankers the same decrepit ones as before, but now bearing new, hastily painted logos.

Jozef had grabbed the opportunity to make money with both hands, increasing the herd and buying milking machines for the dairy, and an Ursus tractor to replace the old jeep. By the time he was thirty the farm was prospering, his sisters married. His mother still cooked, tended the vegetable patch, canned tomatoes and beans from the garden and went to church every Sunday, but since his father had died she hardly spoke. In the evenings they sat together with the television

55

on, but she often seemed to him to be looking somewhere past the screen.

'*Czy znalazłeś żony?*' she asked him quietly every few months, smoothing her apron down nervously and looking past him. 'Have you found a wife?'

At first he had thought that she wanted him to marry, was impatient for it; but as time went on he wasn't so sure whether it was hope behind her question, or fear. And so he waited. The women he knew did not interest him, in any case.

He had voted yes to Europe—they all had. It was a yes to cheap seeds, cheap fertiliser and new markets; why wouldn't he? He filled out form after form about the farm and its yields, laboriously, his mother helping when she could. He took out a loan, modernised the dairy in the way the health officials said he must. He did everything they told him to.

The nearby slaughterhouse was the first to go, unable to cope with the barrage of new regulations. Now Jozef had to send his beef calves away to be killed, and the meat was bought there too. He could no longer sell it in the village, and it was the same for all his neighbours. The market began to dwindle, but a new supermarket came.

Then one of Jozef's neighbours sold up and left for Kraków. Jozef borrowed more money, bought his land and planted wheat.

But then his new dairy failed an inspection. Jozef got a fine, and couldn't pay. The bank foreclosed. It was so quick; one day he was expanding, the next everything, *everything*, was gone. He could not understand what had happened.

He remembered waiting helplessly in the kitchen for his youngest sister to come and collect his mother. She sat at the scarred old table, the same

one he had laid his father on seventeen years
before, turning a box of matches nervously over and
over. When eventually she left she pressed the little
blue box into his big hands and muttered a blessing,
or it could have been a prayer.

A big pork producer—Polish in name, but
linked, so the village said, to America—moved
in and bought Jozef's land. When the first of
the company men arrived to raze the old farm
buildings, they found that the house, with its steeply
pitched roof and weathered cedar shingles, had
already burned almost to the ground.

*   *   *

It was definitely a wolf; the second set of prints
had confirmed it. TC thought hard about where
it could be living and decided it must have a den
somewhere in the woods where the playing fields
met the railway line. There wasn't anywhere else
with enough cover, and besides, there were lots of
squirrels on the common, and probably rats. He
began to comb the woods for fur-filled droppings
or the debris from fresh kills, though he knew the
carcasses themselves would either be eaten or
buried for later. He found more prints, but he did
not search for the den, or for the animal itself; it
was enough to know that it was there, the two of
them inhabiting the same thickets and coverts, his
passing perhaps regarded now and then by grave
yellow eyes.

He was up and out most mornings before Jamal
or his mother were even awake, his tracking book
in his backpack, yesterday's mud still on the knees
of his school trousers. Now, when he climbed his

favourite tree and sat motionless, he often found himself picturing his father's admiration as he told him what he had done. He would bring the wolf to him, somehow, or bring his father to the wolf. And there would be an understanding between the three of them, and it would make his father stay.

When he left school each day the light was already draining from the sky, which bore down, those winter afternoons, like slate. Usually he would go to the common for a bit; sometimes he would go and sit by the railway embankment and watch the trains. The older kids often went to the newsagent or the chicken shop on the high road, so he tended to keep away; or they took their dogs to the little park and hung about on the benches.

TC did not like dogs. Was that true? His mum said he didn't. She told people that he was scared of them, but it was she who walked fast past them and flinched when they sniffed at her. Maybe she was right, though, maybe he didn't like them either. Dogs definitely bit people, and most of the ones on the estate were the fighting kind. TC did not want to stroke them anyway.

One afternoon after school TC found himself wandering north up the high road, away from the little park and the estate. It had rained a thin, icy rain all day and the pavements were wet, and now the bright shop lights were reflected in the puddles under his feet.

Some of the street lights had flashing Christmas decorations strapped to them: stars, a tree, a reindeer, each with its 'Sponsored by . . .' tag. The shops, open late, were a misery of festive music and overheated air.

Last year his dad had taken him to look at the

toys. He had understood that he wasn't to ask for anything, that they were just looking, because sometimes his dad had money and sometimes not, and who knew which it would be by Christmas. But he had picked up one or two things from the shelves and held them a moment before putting them carefully back, his dad asking, 'You like that one, then?' casually, TC nodding casually back. And then on Christmas Day there'd been a big box to unwrap: a monster truck, the exact same kind some of the other boys at school had. They'd taken it out to the yard behind the flats and his dad had driven it around for ages, the whine of its wheels bringing their neighbours up to the windows behind them like shooting targets flipping up. His dad had caught him looking nervously around at them. 'Fuck 'em,' he'd said. 'Jesus, it's Christmas fucking Day.' Yet now, in the toy store, TC found that his eyes seemed to slide off the toys on the shelves; he couldn't get a purchase on them, somehow, or understand what they were about. Maybe the shops were like *EastEnders*; if you stopped keeping track for a bit then none of it made sense and you didn't care anyway. It was just as well, really, he thought, turning and suffering the hot downward blast at the exit.

Outside it was raining again and the pavements were thick with umbrellas and shopping bags banging against hurrying legs. His backpack was too big for him, the straps set too wide apart for his narrow shoulders, and he had to hold them with his hands to keep it on, which made cold rain fall into his cuffs and run towards his elbows. He put his hood up and his head down, picturing the monster truck and how, powered by his dad, it had motored

59

so indefatigably on.

Jamal was at home; he could hear their voices from the stairwell. As he let himself in he heard his mother shout at him from the lounge.

'Oi. Come 'ere.'

TC came to the doorway, his heart thumping.

'You been at my purse?'

Mutely he shook his head.

'Yes you fucking have. You've been stealing off me, you little shit.'

'Hey, hey . . .' This was Jamal, appearing in the kitchen door, a beer in his hand and a dishcloth slung on his shoulder.

'You can fuck off an' all, Jamal, he has, and I ain't having it. What've you got to say for yourself?'

TC listened to his own blood pound in his ears. His eyes felt wide, pinned open. What was the right answer? What was it?

'Well?'

'My dinner money, Mum,' he whispered, looking down at the floor. 'You never leave it out any more.'

For a moment Kelly remained silent and perfectly still. Jamal turned and looked at her, put his beer down. But her eyes slid away from both of them, and she subsided back into the settee.

'Fucking . . . just leave me alone,' she said tiredly, and picked up the remote.

*　　　*　　　*

TC could hear raised voices through the two closed doors between his room and the lounge. It was all so familiar, although now he felt so much older, as though there were years between him and the

60

little boy who had listened to his father and mother fight time and again, and had listened again as his father's feet had thumped away down the stairs.

He thought about what would happen if Jamal left, wondered whether it would be better or worse. Wondered if he would get the blame.

After a while there was a knock at his door. TC jumped and thrust his animal book under the duvet.

'Thought you might want something to eat.' Jamal handed him a plate: sausages and mash. 'Proper mash, that,' he said. 'Not packet.'

TC took the plate and put it on his lap. 'Is there ketchup?'

'Sorry.'

'Doesn't matter.'

The mash was a world away from what they had at school, and TC began to eat. Jamal crouched in front of him, awkwardly, then sat on the bed beside him.

'Look, TC, money's tight for your mum, you know?'

TC said nothing.

'Course she wants you to have your dinner money. You've just got to ask for it, yeah?'

TC looked up, held his gaze. 'Yeah?'

'Yeah, course. I mean, you gotta eat, right?'

'She doesn't care.'

'What? Course she does, kid. She's just . . . things are hard right now, OK?'

'She should get a job, then.'

'Yeah, well, she's trying, but things aren't always that easy.'

'Why not?'

'Because . . . because you can't just walk in somewhere and get a job. It can take a bit of time

61

to find the right one. And anyway, your dad ain't paying either.'

TC put his fork down, went still. 'What do you mean?'

Jamal got up. 'Child support, kid. Your mum's been on to his sister or someone, but apparently he don't want to know. So it ain't all your mum's fault, OK?'

* * *

TC took the dank stairs down two at a time, sobs racking his chest. Outside it was still raining, and he wished he'd grabbed his coat.

He made blindly for the little park and the shelter afforded by the trees behind the benches. One was already occupied; Jozef was smoking a quick cigarette before the start of his evening shift at the takeaway.

TC sat with his knees up on the other bench, swallowing sobs and knuckling his face with his sleeve. Already he was shivering.

Jozef watched the child, careful not to stare. The rain was already making tails and spikes of his dark hair, like an otter's fur. It fell on the back of the boy's neck, and darkened the shoulders of his sweatshirt.

Jozef looked around, but there were no other children, no friends of the boy coming after him; and it was clear that he did not expect anyone to come. Jozef thought of home, how in the village everyone had known him, and how one of their neighbours would have taken him in without question had he ever been found in tears, alone, in the rain.

Yet here, in the city, talking to someone else's child seemed far from simple. But surely the greater wrong would be to walk away, no matter how streetwise the kids here seemed to be, no matter how a grown man talking to a child might look to some. He turned it over in his head: yes, to go to work and leave the little boy alone there on the bench, crying, was unthinkable.

He looked at his scarred hands, took a breath and held it briefly. Then he took his phone out of his pocket and dialled. Across the road he could see Musa pick up.

'Eh, boss,' he said, 'I might be a little bit late. No, I don't know. Sorry.'

When he slipped the phone back in his pocket he saw that the little boy was looking over at him. He wondered how to begin, but, 'You phoned him in the chicken shop, over there,' the boy said.

'Yes.'

'Why?'

'I . . . I want to sit here for a bit.'

'It's raining.'

'I know that. What about you?'

'What?'

'You don't mind the rain?'

'I don't care,' said TC, but by now he was shivering hard.

'Sometimes . . . it is better to be outside, no?'

TC looked away.

'Home is not always good. Sometimes a man needs some fresh air.'

TC nodded.

'That is OK. But sometimes the weather does not agree. Now, my friend at the shop tells me he has made too many chips. Perhaps you could help us

63

out by eating some?' He knew better than to hold
out a hand, or to cajole. The boy studied him for a
moment and then got up.

On the high road the night buses and scooters
and minicabs and stolen motors, the squad cars and
couriers and pizza boys and company cars all halted
for the big Pole and the little boy as together they
crossed the road.

7

PLOUGH MONDAY

Outside the grocer's the fruit was stacked in bright
tiers, their colours improbable in the grey January
light. A man in a grubby apron chased pigeons away
from them with a broom; they lifted from him like
flakes of dull sky, whirled once, and streamed up
the high road to where the lady from the bakery fed
them dustpanfuls of crumbs.

The offices were open again after Christmas, and
the morning buses were full of blank white faces
staring out at Sophia where she sat on one of the
benches in the little park, the drizzle a soft bloom
on her face and hands. The bus windows were
steaming up, full of damp coats and breath, and
Sophia was very glad not to be on one. Growing
old had its compensations, being allowed to please
yourself all day being one of them. It was the first
whole day she had had to herself since Christmas,
and once she had got her doctor's appointment out
of the way she intended to do very little.

She gripped the handle of her stick and got up.

The trees were bare and still, even the ivy's vigour held in temporary abeyance, and only the robin spoke from a sweet chestnut, his song somehow reedier and more subdued than in spring. She paused and looked again at the park, as though committing it to memory, then crossed the grass to the high road and headed slowly north, past the second-hand furniture shop where Denny stood in the doorway with arms crossed, past the chicken takeaway and the betting shop and the post office, its door set between towers of multicoloured buckets and stacking stools and cheap plastic crates.

The pavement—scarred with tarmac, a patchwork of slabs and wounds and make-dos—was a palimpsest, a downtrodden witness to the hardware feeding the street and all its faults and secret requirements. As she walked Sophia pictured the pipes and wires down there beneath her feet, none the less actual for being invisible, like the locket with its tiny diamond chip she had lost in the park twenty years ago and which must have worked its way down into the soil by now, treasure for some future city dweller to find. Perhaps at death she would know what had become of it; perhaps every mystery, every last thing she had ever wondered about or tried to imagine, would be revealed to her. Perhaps that was what heaven was, or would be for her: a lifetime's curiosity about the world finally sated.

Outside the mobile phone shop was tethered a street cleaner's cart, and Sophia had to edge around it, trespassing dizzily into the roaring bus lane. 'Nuisance,' she muttered, but equably enough; she rather admired the little carts, with their neat, no-nonsense practicality, their place for the broom,

65

litter picker and bin bag. They were iconic, in a way; a perfect solution to a problem, and she could recall when the issue of dirty, grimy streets wasn't even addressed. These days they even sent a little ride-on machine at night to steam the chewing gum off. It had whirling brushes at the front, and a mahout to direct it. She had told Daisy about it on one of her visits to the house on Leasow Road, and Daisy had been properly sceptical. 'Who is it that's chewing all the chewing gum, anyway?' she had asked. 'I don't even know one single person that does it.'

Sophia had spent Christmas at Linda's, and it had been very pleasant. She had to admit that the house was lovely, although to her mind it could have done with more books. Linda's taste was very good, and Sophia rather wondered where she got it from; when the children were still at home the flat had been characterised, at least in her memory, by chaos; even in its better moments it may have been clean and neat, but never stylish.

Her daughter's house made her feel careful, although Daisy seemed to treat it fairly cavalierly. The towels were all the same colour, and the saucepans all the same kind. A cleaner came once a week, and between times Linda kept it all very tidy. Even when it wasn't, it wore its disorder elegantly. It was as though the house was allowed to demonstrate what family life could look like, but in a coordinated, artful manner: the good olive oil left out on the sunlit worktop, its cork adrift in a chrism of spilt oil; the Sunday papers strewn over the battered chesterfield; the heirloom doll's house with its contents disordered. At times it reminded Sophia of something in a magazine.

They had had a goose on Christmas Day, not

turkey. There were no fairy lights on the outside of the house, no crackers and no tinsel, which at first she had thought a shame, but then had very much enjoyed making paper chains with Daisy on the day before Christmas Eve. The paper chains came in a special kit, were made of recycled paper and, according to the packaging, helped support women's education in Uganda. Sophia's feelings about this were ambiguous. She eyed the neat stacks of glossy magazines in the recycling box and said nothing.

Daisy was curious and demanding and charming when she least meant to be, although she got away with a lot, which was what happened with only children. Nonetheless, Sophia had always been smitten with her. She had given up on grandchildren by the time Daisy came along; Linda was by then nearing forty, after all, and Michael, twice married and twice divorced, was living in Toronto, and if he was seeing anybody she didn't know about it. She wished Henry could have met Daisy, but at the back of her mind she wondered if the little girl would have loved her quite as much had she also had Henry's doting attention to bask in. He was better with children, always had been; the kids had adored him, and while they loved her, of course, she always felt they treated her with more circumspection. She was not quite as predictable, perhaps; and she had never been one of those mothers who could get down on the floor and play with the children for hours on end. She had loved them both beyond measure, but they had never completely absorbed her in the way that other mothers she had known seemed to be absorbed by their children. Now she was old and these things didn't matter, but back then she had envied Henry his nature walks with Linda and his wrestling matches with Michael, his easy way of being with the children that made them feel special and loved, and her obliquely left out.

As time went on it had seemed that she and Linda were not destined to be close. Everyone said that daughters were difficult, and even as a little girl Linda had been impatient, always wanting things to be different, better—by which she usually meant more like her friends' houses, more like their parents, probably. Yet there wasn't the money for it, and anyway, half of the stuff she wanted was trivial. Books they would have found the money for, if she'd asked. But magazines and make-up didn't matter, not in the long run. She and Henry had stuck to their guns—though it was her mother who Linda most blamed for it at the time. Michael, on the other hand, had been an easy baby and grew up into a sweet-tempered man. She mourned both his divorces, but particularly his first, a Scottish girl he'd been devoted to. He was just like his father in that, for Henry had loved nothing more than when they all did something together, like camping, or a day by the sea. He was a good man, who had loved his family simply, and whom she had adored for every day of their lives together.

When he had the heart attack—in the bathroom, while she was at the council offices complaining about the brutal pollarding of six lime trees outside the flat—her daughter's helpless, illogical anger had beaten Sophia's own tears back before it. She had been too raw, too mired in guilt, to defend herself against the thought that belled at the back of her head and which, quite mistakenly, she ascribed to her daughter and let harden into fact: *It should have been you.*

And so, for the most part, she had done her grieving alone. There had been a moment with Michael, the day after the funeral, when she could have howled; but she knew that the two of them had been discussing who should look after her, and the last thing she wanted was to make Michael stay. His life was in Canada now, and the thought of her children's pity—and later, their resentment—was too much to bear. She had the flat that she and Henry had lived in together, and the trees she loved outside. She would not be a dependant; she would sooner die.

Although hopefully not just yet. After her doctor's appointment she took Glebe Road back, past St Francis's Church with its faded lettering on the gateposts directing carriages where to wait, its 'We need to talk—God' and 'You, me, my place, Sunday!' posters and its noticeboard crowded with well-intentioned activities for the feckless and the elderly. Somebody had dumped a Christmas tree on the pavement outside, and the council was ignoring it. Now it was rusty and brown, the axe marks on its trunk brutally revealed by the flat January light.

The doctor had said they wanted to run some tests. For a while now her heart had been skipping beats; she pictured it fluttering briefly in the cage of her chest, and then quieting again. She felt all right, apart from that, and there was no sense in worrying Linda; in any case, a conversation about heart problems, given Henry, was more than she could face. It was probably nothing; age came with all sorts of inconveniences and frailties, most of which were better ignored.

At the door of her block she noted with approval that the stunted old quince was struggling into bloom, its waxy coral flowers for now locked in tight little fists. She loved the way they unfurled on the bare black branches long before the leaves came out, reminding her every year of kimonos. Bees loved them, too, and there was precious little else about for them this early in the year.

You could buy insect hotels these days, and special bee nests; she had seen it on TV. Henry would have called it faddy. What they wanted was a woodpile, or failing that a compost heap; one they could get into, not those plastic bins like big black Daleks. She wished she could have one in the little park, somewhere for her potato peelings and tea bags, and for the clippings she stuffed in her pocket while she was surreptitiously doing the rounds with her secateurs.

Sophia cut the thought off, because to indulge it was to entertain a whole list of wishes, from a mixed border along the back wall of the estate to a cold frame, some bird boxes and a half-hundredweight of wild-flower seeds. Instead, she let herself into the flat and switched the radio on for company.

Yesterday Daisy had given her a letter, with strict instructions not to read it until she got home. There it was on the kitchen table, and once she had put the shopping away Sophia sat down to read it.

At four o'clock she made tea: a clean tea cloth on the tray, the brown teapot, the Cornish jug, two biscuits on a worn plate that had once had flowers on and still did, in Sophia's mind. Outside, starlings, their individual ribaldry lost in the solemn mystery of the flock, wheeled and bellied and folded over the little park before sweeping west and pouring down on the oaks on the common to roost, as they did every winter evening, a daily urban miracle that went almost completely unremarked.

Once it was over, Sophia took the tray to the sitting room, switched on the little lamp by her favourite chair and settled down to read. By six it was getting dark; 'dimmity', Henry would have called it. It was the hour when foxes began to materialise in the streets outside, neat sepia shapes that flickered silently at the edges of the local dogs' knowing and haunted the margins of their dreams. Sophia got up to do the washing-up and stood for a moment, her hands in the sink, looking past her reflection at the dim outlines of the trees and the bright traffic beyond. She thought about the dying of the light, and in her mind's eye she saw Henry on the bathroom floor, his dear eyes closed, his big heart stilled, his pepper-and-salt stubble unrinsed from the washbasin for the first and only time in their lives together.

It was late when she went to bed, somewhere between *Book at Bedtime* and the midnight news. Outside she could hear shouts, a burst of drunken song: kicking-out time. January, she thought. Soon enough it will be screams. But it was foxes she was thinking of: the vixens would soon start looking for mates, and the unearthly sounds of their clicketting would haunt the park outside her window for weeks.

In the night Sophia woke, swimming slowly up through sleep like a bubble through black oil. One by one she assumed control of each of the elements of her dream, until at last she was not dreaming it, but thinking.

Awake in the dark room, beached in her too-big

bed, she pictured the country stretching out around her in the dark: the West Country far away beyond the bedroom window, Scotland off somewhere to her right. She pictured it quiet and sleeping, herself but a frail, passing creature, lost in the vastness of the familiar land mass and the even greater vastnesses beyond.

*　　　*　　　*

Musa often seemed to be on a cigarette break when the boy called in at the takeaway. At first Jozef wondered whether TC waited for him to disappear from behind the counter before coming in, or whether Musa somehow didn't like the kid, and was avoiding him; eventually he realised the taciturn little Turk was making it easier for him to give the boy food.

'Nobody cook at home tonight?' he asked, as TC appeared diffidently at the counter for the third evening in a row. TC shook his head; Jamal did cook when he came round, but he wasn't there all the time.

There was nowhere to sit in the takeaway, but TC lingered at the counter, making the chips last. It was clear to Jozef that he didn't want to go home.

'Eh, kid,' he said. 'You play chess?'

TC shook his head.

'You want to learn?'

He went to the back room and retrieved a stool for TC, put it in front of the counter. From his holdall he fetched the chess set he'd found in the old man's house; he often took it to the Polish cafe after his shift for a game. Musa, appearing behind the counter, raised an eyebrow at him. 'It's quiet,

72

boss,' said Jozef. 'Nobody here. If customers come I stop playing, OK?'

*   *   *

The dog had been gone for weeks, and Jozef no longer whistled for her when he cut through the little park or across the common. Yet as he walked back from the Polish cafe that night, warm from the cherry vodka they'd given him, there she was at his side, grinning and steadfast, her flat head as soft as satin under his hand. *'Gdziety ty byłaś, Znajda?'* he whispered, crouching down to look her over. But wherever she had been she did not seem harmed, and Jozef was surprised by the strength of his relief. 'Znajda! Znajda!' he called out, and broke into a run, the dog jumping and bounding joyfully at his side.

They jogged the length of the common together, the exercise and the cold night air chasing the alcohol from Jozef's blood. The night was clear, the moon keeping pace with them through the black branches and turning the grass silver, illuminating their twin trails through the dewfall where they ran.

All around them, the common was alive: the brambles full of roosting songbirds, the little copse stalked by foxes and the leaf litter rustling with voles, hunted, now and then, by a kestrel who had a nest high on a housing block three streets away. It was intoxicating and familiar; it smelled of new life and decay, and though bound about by roads and regulations Jozef understood then that it was a wild place, and not subject to anyone or anything at all.

As they neared the road they slowed, and it came to Jozef that he did not want to take Znajda back to

73

Denny and the dark little room above the shop. He rested his hands on his knees and looked at her, his breath forming brief clouds in front of his face. The dog sprawled blissfully on the wet grass at his feet and smiled.

* * *

At first, Musa did not want to let Jozef leave the dog at the takeaway.

'Please. Just one night,' repeated Jozef. 'I pick her up tomorrow, I swear.'

'Joe, you should take her back to Denny, you know,' replied Musa; but his hand was gently massaging her scarred ears. 'Is his dog. He gonna breed from her again soon.'

'He makes her live upstairs, Musa, he never even walk her. You know that.'

Musa shook his head. 'You think you can keep her secret, my friend? Where will you go? She can't stay here.'

'I'll find a new place to live,' Jozef replied, realising suddenly that he should have done so a long time ago. 'I'll ask around tomorrow. I don't want to work for Denny no more, anyway.'

'Where will you get money, then?' asked the little Turk; but he already knew what Jozef would say next.

The second-hand furniture shop was dark when Jozef got back, the stairs unlit. He let himself into his room and switched on the light. He had lived there for months, but it bore barely any trace of him at all.

He lay on the bed and stared at the ceiling. It would be good to find some extra work to supplement his money from the takeaway; he would definitely need more cash, even with the extra shifts Musa had given him. At least he had not gambled away his wages for the last couple of weeks.

A little bedsit would do fine. Somewhere warm where he and Znajda could sleep and where he could cook for himself. He would buy his own sheets and towels, kitchen things; he'd walk Znajda every morning, and find new places for them to explore at the weekends.

The mattress with its dent was like the shallow scrape a hare makes in a field, and as he lay there Jozef was reminded of his dream. He could already imagine the coiled and graceful musculature of the hare he would carve; but first he would finish the creature he had begun. He got up and went to the window. There it was on the sill, smiling up at him. He picked it up and ran his thumb over it, picturing how Znajda's strong chest would push bravely out of the wood, and how her broad head with its soft ears would acquire a patina over time.

The pigeons lined up fat and flea-ridden on the ledges across the street regarded the yellow window for a moment, where behind the glass a big man leaned on the sill and began to coax a dog's form from an end of old wood.

8

CANDLEMAS

January had been dull and mild. But as the new year wore on, the temperatures dropped, and the month went out on a hard frost which silvered the city from the suburbs to its asphalt heart. By the afternoon of 1 February the lawns had thawed, but that night the frost came again, and the next day they stayed white until nightfall. And each night after that the frost drove deeper and deeper down into the ground.

First the puddles in the park formed a thin skin of ice, then a rocking lid; a few more days into February and they were solid, even the mud around them frozen hard under the dog walkers' feet. Beside the railway embankment the brambles' dauntless leaves looked suddenly limp and drab.

Along Leasow Road ice had bound the gravel on the driveways so that it no longer gave so readily underfoot. In pots and front gardens the last surviving pelargoniums now drooped bletted and blackening; the north-facing back gardens, deprived even of the cold sun, were claimed utterly, the frost reaching even to the dankest, most sheltered corners. Only a few early snowdrops raised their heads from the frozen ground.

The birds became bold; hundreds were lost to the ammil every night, and hunger drove them to new braveries with each unrelenting day. They froze where they slept in the hedges and trees, their bodies falling secretly to the ground like leaves. They were merely feet and feathers, hardly a mouthful for the city's sleek cats and opportunistic foxes.

*   *   *

Monday was Bristol, and a dim, early start. Linda hurried to her car with her arms crossed, each breath forming a cloud that hung in the still air even after she had moved through it. In the car she turned the heating up full and decided against removing her coat, although she knew that halfway there she'd be uncomfortable. She thrust her hands between her knees for a moment, her shoulders hunched, leg muscles taut against the icy air of the footwell. Something crackled in her coat pocket: her mother's letter to Daisy. She had had supper with them the night before, only remembering to give Linda the letter on the short drive back to the estate.

Something about her mother's visit rankled. What was it? Idly, she turned it over in her mind; there was always something. That was it: Daisy's school project. 'Is it all right if I help Daisy at the weekend?' Sophia had asked. 'Or does it have to be handed in before then?' It wasn't that she hadn't known about the 'Our Seasons' project, just that she hadn't realised Daisy had asked her grandmother for help. She must have looked surprised. 'Well, love, you mustn't mind. You're not a very outdoors person,' her mother had said.

Impatiently she stuffed the letter in the glovebox, and tuned the radio to a talk station to keep her company on the long drive. The weather report sounded like an incantation against the gods.

In town she drove aggressively, but without the

77

fine judgement to back it up. She knew all the routes out of the city well, and she was confident in her choices, but she wasn't good at anticipating other drivers and once or twice had to brake hard; several times she chose to cut people off, dealing with it simply by refusing to meet the other driver's eyes.

Once she was on the motorway and clear of the city she began to relax. The sun had begun to throw the trees' shadows long across the silver fields, and by nine it was warming the left side of her face. The sky was a theatre of clouds, the hard shoulders patrolled by pairs of crows, and red kites wheeled overhead, riding the road's rising thermals in wide, sweeping curves.

The frost was disappearing fast from the flanks of the fields facing the sun, though it lingered in the lees and in the pockets. Where it had gone, the fields were mostly ridged and brown, although one or two were baized with green. Linda wondered vaguely what could be growing in them at this time of year—weeds, perhaps.

In a few of the fields left fallow, wrecked lorries acted as makeshift advertising hoardings. One was fashioned from an old shipping container which had been gently collapsing for several years. It was for a debt-collection agency, although the telephone number, with its outdated dialling code, was now partly missing. Below it the sheltered field was grazed by sheep, lit golden, as the sun crested the rise, like a Constable pastoral.

She pulled over because something hit the windscreen, and once she had stopped she found she was shaking. What the hell was it? She thought she had seen feathers, a brief flash of black and white like a subliminal message thumping on the glass, but what on earth would a bird be doing flying around on the motorway? But then, they were notoriously stupid, flying into aeroplanes' engines and the like. The windscreen wasn't damaged, anyway, and for that she was grateful.

Whatever it was it had gone; there was no dead bird anywhere that she could see. Linda got out of the car, pulling her coat around her, and took a breath. The motorway was busy, and she turned her back on the lorries thundering past. On the other side of the crash barrier was a wood, the winter trunks faintly green with algae. Some of the trees were lagged with ivy, the trunks teacosied in glossy leaves, the branches jutting bare.

Something moved deep in the trees. Linda peered in, but could make nothing out. There it was again: a little brown bird running up a trunk like a mouse. It circled around the trunk, moving out of view. *Not an outdoor person*, she thought, bipping the car doors locked and stepping over the barrier into the wood.

Beyond the tangle of saplings and undergrowth at its margins the wood was trackless, but dry underfoot: there was a thick covering of brown leaves and little husks on the ground, and few plants grew between the smooth trunks. Almost immediately, the roar of the motorway receded behind her.

To Linda's surprise, it was more than just a windbreak for the road. She had expected a field on the other side, but after a couple of minutes' walking she was still surrounded by trees. What was the point of it? It didn't look as though people were cutting it for timber, and it was too close to the motorway for paintballing. She wondered if it had a name, and who it belonged to. At least there was no danger of getting lost. The sound of the traffic was still a dull hum behind her; she could follow it back to the car any time she liked.

She knew that what she was doing was out of character, but perhaps that was the point. 'You'll never guess what I did today,' she'd say to Steven that night, when she got in. How surprised he'd be, and who could blame him? But, 'Nothing wrong with a walk in the woods, sweet pea,' her father would have said. She could see him now, striding in front of her in his long black coat. And if she put her foot down she could still be in Bristol on time.

She pushed on, and it began to seem as though she was in another world. The trees had closed around her, and for a moment she felt that the wood could well go on forever, in all directions, her imaginary map of the country covered with an ancient tangled darkness instead of the straight lines of her car journeys. Of course it wasn't so, but she stopped anyway and listened for the distant, reassuring sound of the traffic. Was that it? She wasn't sure. Yet she hadn't walked for very long; it should be easy enough to find the car again.

All around her the smooth grey trunks reached up straight and leafless to the sky, the ground beneath mulched in russet leaves. Yet something near her foot snagged her eye. Pushing through the leaf litter was a tiny green shoot, with all the unmistakable energy of a bulb. Once she had seen one, she saw they were everywhere. It came to her from somewhere that felt like childhood that these were bluebells, and that in a couple of months this tiny, forgotten corner of woodland would be a paradise, the cars speeding by unheeding as the wood performed a miracle entirely of its own making, designed only for itself and for no human eyes at all. She wondered if anybody in the entire world knew it but her.

Back on the hard shoulder the car ticked as it cooled. The GPS on the dashboard reflected the sky; in the glovebox was Sophia's reply to her granddaughter, a clutch of black honesty seeds in their milky discs sleeping in its folds.

*   *   *

What had begun with a few grey clouds chasing their shadows across the fields had become a legion, and the sky was heavy and dull. A flock of lapwings, nearly a thousand of them, took off as one from a field in which the winter wheat was just coming through, their broad, blunt wings flashing white and black as they turned. They had arrived nearly six weeks ago, riding a north-easterly from Scandinavia, to eat insects and invertebrates on the Somerset Levels, just as they had been doing for time out of mind—although the big flocks, tens of thousands strong, were a rarity these days. They wheeled and resettled further upwind as Linda emerged from the beech hanger into the field and turned to toil back along the field margin to the road. The wind picked up, gusting over the contours of the frozen land, and brought with it the smell of snow.

*   *   *

In the city it was simply another miserable winter day. Home time: TC decided against going to the common because of the cold. Craning up from the street he could see the lounge light was off; that meant his mum was out and it was OK to watch TV and mess around.

The flat was dark and cold when he let himself in, but he switched the fire on and soon the lounge was warm enough. He made himself toast and found a Coke in the fridge, and sprawled on the settee. It would be brilliant to live all by yourself, he thought. You could do anything you wanted. You could watch TV all night or never, ever wash, and nobody could say anything.

You'd smell, though. He hoped he didn't smell. Did he smell? It was one of those things other kids said, but that didn't mean it was true. How often did people wash their clothes? he wondered. It would be easier if they had a washing machine. Or if he had more clothes. Who cared, anyway. He did wash, every day. And did his teeth. He'd even bought the toothpaste. Well, he'd stolen it, but it was the same thing.

In olden times nobody brushed their teeth or washed every day. Yeah, but they got plague and all their teeth fell out. It would be awful to have false teeth. Or bad breath. He hoped he didn't have bad breath. If he were to breathe on someone—if someone came close enough. What happened if you lived in the wilderness, like doing survival? You didn't get to wash all the time then. You must just stink. Or maybe you stopped after a bit, like if you don't wash your hair it starts cleaning itself. His dad would've been able to tell him; his dad had been out on manoeuvres. You didn't care about washing in the army.

Or maybe after a while you just stopped being

able to smell yourself. That would be awful—if you stank and you didn't know it. Did he stink? He sniffed his armpits; they smelled warm and close. It wasn't horrible—was it?—but it was something.

Maybe he should go to the launderette. But that cost money. He could save up his lunch money, if maybe that man would give him lunch. Jozef. But the other kids went to the takeaway at lunch; he couldn't. And anyway, he'd been getting too much free food off him recently; it was probably a bit weird. His dad would've put a stop to it, TC was sure. 'What's in it for him?' he'd've asked, and told TC to wise up, not to be so trusting. But then, he wasn't here.

*　　*　　*

That evening it began to snow. It drifted down all night, and in the morning the schools were closed. Steven was freelance and worked from home, but the road outside was ungritted and treacherous, and so Linda had a rare day off.

The garden had looked so perfect when she first woke up. Everything seemed hushed, for one thing; the world holding its breath. The lawn was perfectly level, even the tallest grass blades covered, the fence posts each topped with a white loaf, the shrubs sugary and hunched.

Before long the silence was broken by shrieks and squeals as the neighbourhood children tumbled out into the snow. Daisy pleaded strenuously to be allowed to play in the street, but you couldn't be too careful, said Linda, not with the estates all around. They watched her play in the garden instead; Steven showed her how to squeeze a snowball so

83

that it stuck, and they built the obligatory snowman, and it quickly began to look churned up and messy.

There were no buses all day and few trains. With no official word on what to do the city awarded itself a holiday, although the recriminations—the lost revenue, the lack of snowploughs, the inevitable safety issues—would come thick and fast later on. So the short winter's day had no rhythm; no rush hour topped or tailed it, and it was only as the light failed and the cold regripped the air that the grimy, misshapen snowmen were abandoned, and the snowballers, feet cold, hands numb, retreated indoors from the treacherous and darkening streets.

At five o'clock the winter afternoon reached that brief fulcrum when the sky outside takes on a deep, almost luminous blue, lasting for just a few minutes before shading into dark; Linda, gazing out of the living-room window, hesitated to turn on the lights lest they drive out the last remaining light from the sky. Candles were what a day like today called for, but the only ones in the house were perfumed, and ruinously expensive. To hell with it, she thought, and fetched the Cook's matches from the kitchen. It wasn't as though they couldn't afford more. Daisy was upstairs on her computer, her gloves and hat steaming gently on the radiator, and it was time for Linda to start thinking about supper. Drawing the curtains and turning away from the window, she thought about the day before.

The first few flakes had drifted down while she was in Bristol. Driving back the sky had been a dull orange either side of the bypass, the flakes whirling dizzily in her headlamps, and for one brief stretch of road the street lights flickered on pair by pair on either side, keeping pace with her car as though to light her way and her way alone.

She had been so tired when she got home that she hadn't even mentioned her walk, and now it seemed too late to bring it up. Besides, what was there to tell? She had walked into a wood for no reason at all, and afterwards she had not wanted to get back into the car. It was hardly much of an anecdote, although an image, detailed and finely drawn, of a secret carpet of bluebells had remained at the back of her mind all day.

*   *   *

Sophia sat at her kitchen table with a whisky soda and watched the snow in the little park turn briefly pink as the last light drained from the sky. On the paths it was becoming compacted into ice, and she knew that if it froze tonight they would be impassable for her tomorrow, stick or no stick. Still, she had a cupboard full of tins and a bottle of excellent Scotch, and doubtless Linda would call to check she wasn't doing anything daring or ill-advised.

She wondered if Daisy was enjoying the snow— if Linda was letting her. There was no after-school club for playing in the snow, no educational aspect either. That was part of its magic: that for once the streets would be full of children released briefly from the strictures of their daily routines, outside with no purpose at all but to kick about and have fun together, as children should. Tough city kids were rendered giggling and silly; protected middle-class children were gifted with brief freedom by the temporary saturnalia of snow.

85

Yes, a spell of real winter was a good thing. Another generation would be able to remember proper snow, inches deep, and in a while it might come to seem to them as though every winter had been like this one. Anyway, a good freeze was just what the bulbs needed, and it would help kill off the pests so that things would grow well next spring.

*   *   *

Jozef waited by the benches, his arms folded against the cold, the chess set inside his jacket pressing hard against his chest. He needed to get some warmer clothes, that was for sure. It was almost as cold as Poland. His father had always seemed to know when the first big snowfall was coming and would get the herd in just in time, but after he died Jozef found he hadn't the knack. He lost a heifer that first winter; the melting snow revealed it in March, huddled against a wall like a hide stretched over a frame. Its eyes had been neatly picked out by crows.

What with the snow and the schools shut it had been a quiet shift: chicken boxes, as usual, the mad old Jamaican man and his hot wings. The boy had turned up again, slinking in sometime after lunch. He'd bought nuggets and had insisted on giving Jozef two pounds, which Jozef had ostentatiously rung up. TC had grinned and demanded the receipt; Jozef was pleased by the grin, and how it transformed the boy's solemn little face. He was going to be good-looking in a few years, with his dark eyes and long lashes. He already was.

Jozef had taken a room in Musa's cousin's flat, and had put it about among the people he knew that he was looking for a place of his own. Emir drove a cab and was out most of the time, but when he was in he tolerated Znajda well enough. She would follow him from room to room when he got up in the morning, the stump of her tail wagging. He would make her sit for his toast crusts.

After his shift he had taken Znajda for a quick run around on the common, so she would be OK for the evening in the flat by herself. Now he was waiting for the boy to come. He was going to take him to the Polish cafe, see if he could get a good meal into him—something wholesome, something that wasn't fried. *Bigos*, maybe; it was the right weather for stew. But the boy was already more than half an hour late; perhaps he wouldn't come at all. Jozef looked at his watch and decided to give it another ten minutes. Fifteen at most.

The street lights flickered on, turning the churned-up snow sodium orange. With so little moving either by road or rail, the night-time city grew eerily quiet, while high above the blanketed roofs and black branches hung the deadening sky where cargo upon cargo of flakes pressed and were held and awaited their silent release.

9

SHROVETIDE

The snow lasted a week and was chased away by cold February drizzle. The snowmelt sang secretly in the gutters, and before long all that remained was the odd dirty hillock to mark where a snowman had been.

Jozef was working the lunchtime shift, the counter crowded with kids in and out of uniform all wanting their Junior Specials, tinny dancehall blaring from their phones. They were aggressive, loud and quick to take offence; nothing like he had been at that age. They had such confidence, such a sense of entitlement. It was as though the world existed for them and them alone, and nobody else counted; yet also, in their defensiveness, as though they might not count at all, as though everything, every interaction, was a battle to be won. Were all British children like that, he wondered, or just the city ones? Perhaps, one day, he would take a trip, go and see the rest of the island. Parts of it, he'd heard, were beautiful. Little villages, churches, farms. Perhaps one day he would see them. There had to be more to it than this.

The shifts at the takeaway were gruelling and relentless, but he had made up his mind that it would not be for long. Every morning he went through the papers. There were jobs, but nothing any better than the takeaway, and his English could do with being a bit better. Plus he'd probably have to pay tax. Perhaps it was better to stay on, put the money by. For now.

At lunchtime he took Znajda out for a walk. As he cut through the little park the old ash tree made him think of home, and he reached out to touch its rough bark as he passed.

On the other side of the common was a broad, straight road, once a turnpike. It was lined with horse chestnuts which in spring were like thunderheads candled with creamy flowers; now, though, the leaves were still held in tight buds. Znajda trotted ahead of him, ears up. She often saw squirrels there.

Then, from nowhere, there was TC, running and stumbling from a side road, something about his gait stopping Znajda in her tracks. Jozef heard hoots and calls, and a half-empty drinks can spun past TC's head and landed near Znajda, who gave a low growl. TC saw the dog and froze, but it was not him she was growling at. He backed past her and straight into Jozef, and they both watched as Znajda advanced towards three teenage boys who had rounded the corner, her lips drawn back to show her teeth. One boy, Jozef saw, was picking up a stone.

'Hey,' he called out, as the dog unleashed a torrent of barks, 'I would not do that, my friend.' He stepped forward to stand beside Znajda. 'One word from me, she kill you.' It was not hard to believe; the normally peaceable Znajda was transformed, her low growl even enough to give Jozef pause. The kids slunk off, calling jeers over their shoulders once they judged themselves far enough away.

It was easy to see why TC had drawn the older boys' attention; he had twigs in his hair and the knees of his trousers were green. To Jozef he looked like a *leszy*, a woodland spirit. He itched to dust down the boy's hair, but did not want to spook him further.

'You OK?' he asked. TC nodded. 'You sure?' He nodded again, his eyes drifting to Znajda. 'Don't worry about her, she won't hurt nobody,' said Jozef, wondering if it was true. Yet she was her phlegmatic self again, sitting in her lopsided fashion and waiting for her walk to continue.

Although TC looked unsure about the dog, he

89

didn't seem about to leave either. Jozef thought he understood. 'You are going this way? Good. You mind we walk with you?' TC shook his head. 'This is Znajda,' he explained. 'It means found one; orphan.'

'Is it yours?'

Jozef hesitated. 'Yes, I think so. She was lost, for a while, but she came back—to me.'

'Is it a pit bull?'

Jozef's big hands, scarred now from hot fat as well as the awl, were kneading the dog's ears with infinite gentleness. 'No. She's very friendly dog, most of the time. I think she didn't like those boys, though.'

'Yeah!' said TC, breaking into a grin. 'You see the way she growled at them! She's fierce. She can do *anything*.' Hearing herself praised, Znajda put her ears back for a fuss, but TC kept his hands in his pockets.

'No school today?' asked Jozef.

TC looked down. 'Teacher training.'

Jozef considered the boy's uniform and said nothing.

'Were you on your way to the chicken shop?' TC asked, transparently.

*　　　*　　　*

They took their chips to the benches in the little park. Jozef put his collar up against the cold.

'So you think it was my Znajda's footprints you saw?' he asked.

TC nodded. 'If there'd been footprints as well— you know, people's footprints—I would've known it was a dog, but it was just one set so I didn't even

90

think of it.'

'It's possible. She was lost for a long time. But where do you think she was living?'

'On the common somewhere, I reckon. Do you think she can catch her own food?'

Jozef looked down at her; she was cracking a fried-chicken bone nonchalantly between her back teeth. 'Maybe she wouldn't have to.'

'Bins . . . that's true.'

'I hope you are not too disappointed.'

TC thought for a moment. He knew he should be, but somehow it didn't seem to matter quite as much as it had. He shook his head.

'So what did you think it was?' Jozef asked. 'Something more exciting than my Znajda, yes?'

'Yeah . . .' TC hesitated, then looked up at Jozef's face. 'Like . . . like a wolf, maybe,' he said, and was surprised to find it felt OK to say it. 'An escaped one. There are panthers out there, all sorts. People see them all the time. A man got bit by a big cat in Luton last year, taking his bins out, I saw it.'

'Ah. Well then, that is not so crazy. And anyway, all dogs come from wolves. That means Znajda is almost a wolf; so you were almost right.'

TC finished his chips and began folding his napkin up very precisely. 'Ain't no wolves here, though.'

'Maybe not,' replied Jozef. 'But you know, there are wolves where I come from. Poland. In the forests of the north are wolves still.'

'You ever seen one?'

'No. But I have been to the forests. I think the wolves have probably seen me.'

TC looked up, his napkin now a tiny triangle

91

like a folded flag, his eyes wide. He looked at Jozef properly for the first time, this man known to wolves.

Jozef handed him his own napkin. 'Where did you learn to do that?'

'My dad.' But he did not fold Jozef's, instead getting up and putting them both, with the greasy boxes, in the bin.

'Thank you,' came a voice from behind them. It was an old lady, leaning on a stick.

'What for?'

'Putting the rubbish in the bin. Lots of boys don't.'

TC regarded her for a moment with his dark eyes. She smiled to show no criticism was about to follow, but with a quick 'Bye, mister' to Jozef, he turned and was gone.

She came and sat beside Jozef. 'He is not your boy.'

'No. He comes to the takeaway often.'

Znajda sniffed at her stick with precise and thorough interest.

'He plays truant, you know. Misses school.'

'Yes. But what can you do.'

She looked at him speculatively. 'Indeed. It is not easy. And you? I see you here sometimes.'

'I work at the takeaway. Jozef.'

'I am Sophia. You are Polish?'

'Yes.'

'Do you like it here?'

'Yes, I do. Now is cold, but in summer it's very beautiful.'

'It is, isn't it. I'm so glad you think so. Such a *green* city, even around here. So many trees.'

'It's true. So big, so old. And many different

92

ones.'

'Did you know, from this bench you can see eleven different species? Eleven. Think of it.'

'That is very many. I can see . . . *dąb*, that is one.'

'Oak,' said Sophia quietly, and smiled.

'*Jarząb pospolity*—' he pointed at the rowan—'that is two; *klon jawor*, three—what do you call that one, in English?'

'Sycamore,' said Sophia. 'How funny, it rhymes.'

'And that one, that one is my favourite, I call it *jesion wyniosły . . .*'

'Ah, the tree of the world. Mine too. I take it you are from the countryside yourself? Not a city?'

'Yes. A small village. Many farms. Today, though, it is all EU, you know? They want to make it like one big farm. All the small farmers, they have to leave. They do not understand the rules, or they cannot afford changes, they get inspection, they get a big fine, too big, and then—' he clicked his fingers—'*koniec*. It is over.'

'That is very sad. You miss home?'

'Yes,' said Jozef, simply. 'I miss it.'

'Well, you should be working outdoors, at the very least. You are still a farmer, after all. Aren't you? I expect the council would be glad of you.'

'Council? To do what job?'

'In the parks. You know, upkeep. Planting bulbs. Tree felling. Whatever it is they do.'

The image made his heart leap, but it was too easy. He looked down at his hands, then away.

*   *   *

Outside the West African restaurant the rusting Victorian gaslights were hung with palms and

93

little calabashes. 'Good Lord,' muttered Sophia as she passed, and wondered what the long-dead lamplighter would have made of it.

It quite put her off her train of thought. She was on the way to the shops, repeating the things she needed to buy under her breath. She despised lists.

'Scotch,' she began, starting with the most important. 'Ritz crackers. Writing paper. Flour.' A black-and-white dog tethered outside the cab office wagged its tail hopefully as she passed. 'Fairy. Eggs. Lenor.' Surely there had been more. Bugger the calabashes. 'Aha! *Reader's Digest*!' She looked around in triumph.

Henry used to bring the papers home every day, but nowadays she found they were just too much. Travel, cars, sport—half of it usually went straight in the bin, she just didn't have the time. And the adverts! As she grew older she found they seemed to be written in a kind of code that had no currency with her. Yet they remained alluring: as insidious as petrol and just as dangerous. You could look away, of course, but it took willpower, and not everyone was as stubborn as she was. It was the kids she worried about most, always being told to want things, rarely being shown how *not* to, which, after all, was the trick. Yes, age came with many benefits, and she was glad to be no longer in the admen's sights.

She got her news from the radio these days, if she wanted any, and the local paper that got pushed through the door. Half the time it was just upsetting, though, the way things seemed to be going wrong. You couldn't do anything about any of it; the next lot would just have to fend for themselves, just like they had. Better not to leave it too buggered up for them, but it was probably too late anyway.

Henry's cronies had been given to complaining that the young ones had it all too easy—no national service, no world war. What rot. They had bigger problems even than that to contend with: they had to stop everything from really going to hell. Sometimes she felt she could weep to think of how all the lovely places would probably be lost: felled, flooded, poisoned, built over. Sometimes she was just glad she wouldn't be around long enough to see it. Yes, she was a member of the last generation to have been able to live really recklessly, using what they wanted and throwing it away. Now innocence was lost, and there was no point pretending you didn't know what having all this stuff really cost.

But nobody could save the world all by themselves. All anyone could really do was stick to what they thought was important, in a small way, and hope it rubbed off. And it didn't always. Look at Linda: you wouldn't have thought she had the father she did. When she was young Henry had taught her what all the different trees were, and the flowers, and the constellations, which just went to show that what you thought was worth knowing didn't always take. Michael, on the other hand, was a different matter. But he was on the other side of the world.

Sophia sighed and began to cross the road. At least there was Daisy. Which reminded her: she had to get something for her birthday. What was it Linda had said she wanted? Damned if she'd phone her to ask. There'd be something perfectly nice in the local shops, she thought. There usually was.

10

WINNOL WEATHER

March blew in soft and damp. The snowdrops were over, but there were plenty of crocuses in the front gardens still, some blazing like candles of yolky tallow and royal purple, some limp, their heavy heads collapsed, drained by their leaves which were coming up fast around them. Overhead, high clouds scudded over on a smart breeze.

After school TC went to look for owl pellets in the woods which bordered the railway tracks. Nothing; there probably weren't any. He'd never even heard an owl, after all.

He made his way to the place where a huge fallen tree crossed the path and climbed to the top of its perpendicular root ball. The trunk had been sawn into sections, but apart from a gap for the path it had been left where it fell; most of its bark had long rotted off, and one segment was tagged with red graffiti: 'mary jane'; 'tree land', oddly; the ubiquitous cock and balls. TC looked down at the ground beneath him and thought about how it was the surface of the earth, how if he were to climb down and lay his hand on the path, right now, he would be touching the very skin of the planet.

The brambles formed a dull, purplish carpet beneath the trees, but at the paths' margins was the fresh green of the new season's cow parsley and nettles, still just a few inches tall. The undergrowth was alive with birds: magpies calling *ch-chack* from the branches, blackbirds, heads cocked, listening for worms in the leaf litter, robins bustling across the paths. After the long winter they were suddenly voluble, singing out the fact of their survival and laying claim to territories for spring.

Walking back from the common TC pressed the button at the crossing by the station and waited for the lights. People massed around him off the train, purposeful and harried with their bags and mobile phones; you only saw that type twice a day, and TC wondered where they went the rest of the time. Offices, he supposed. He tried to picture what that would be like, and failed.

A man in a suit started out across the road and TC went after him, not thinking, but the lights had changed and a lorry leaned on its horn and TC had to run, heart kicking, eyes wide. The traffic snarled behind him; more horns, then, and a bang. TC didn't look back.

*   *   *

A brisk March breeze blew Sophia's thin hair about her head. Daisy was coming over after school, and she was returning from the shops where she had bought fish fingers and oven chips for their tea, against Linda's specific instructions.

The hawthorn hedge near the tall tower blocks was studded with tiny green buds, and the lone ash had black knots on the end of its pendulous twigs. Over the coming months they would swell and become sticky before bursting late into leaves that looked far too fresh for a tree with such a riven, twisted trunk. As Sophia passed it she tapped it for luck with her stick. Also made of ash, she thought, as a siren wailed distantly behind her. Perhaps they had once known each other. Silly woman.

In the little park, last year's leaves were the merest of brown tatters littering the grass, sinking towards the roots where the worms would take them down so they could slowly rot to make soil. And from that soil would come more leaves, and then more, long after she had died. She wondered when that would be, but curiously, not morbidly. As each year cycled past she was aware there was a dark corollary to her birthday somewhere along its line: her death day, through which she passed, unremarked, year after year.

Back at home she hid the shopping away in case Linda broke from habit and came in. She had tried to persuade her daughter that Daisy was perfectly fine walking the few hundred yards from school on her own—which wasn't really on her own anyway, but with dozens of other children—but to no avail.

More sirens. As she looked out of the window she felt like a mother again—not that she wasn't still, that was silly, but for a moment it was as though she were waiting for Linda and Michael to come home from school. The kids had loved the estate then, hadn't known enough to be critical of it; not that Sophia herself had failed to see its growing problems, but her disappointment had always been tempered with love, and with pragmatism.

Only the little park around the estate, with its legacy of grand Victorian trees, had remained more or less the same. She had always loved it—Henry, too—but after the children left home it had become even more important to her. It was hard to say why she felt such responsibility for it; perhaps because Henry had loved it, perhaps because nobody else seemed to bother about it, not even the council, not really. She had begun picking up litter and, later, planting seeds; it gave her a purpose. And it proved such a consolation after he died that, now, she considered it more or less her own.

Would that Henry had had the chance to enjoy it with her. When the factory closed he was only a few years off retirement; he had taken it hard, but then had found work at the little garden centre nearby, and had found that he loved it. 'I wish I'd done it years ago,' he'd laughed, as though it had been a choice he'd made rather than a circumstance that had terrified him at the time.

He was good at it, too; he'd had an allotment for years, and he had a gentle way with the customers. 'Sometimes it's like they're scared of the plants,' he'd say. 'They've lost touch, you see. I tell 'em, "That plant wants to live, see, and he knows how even if you don't. He'll be all right—unless you really mess him about, that is." '

Of course, it wasn't for long. There was no reason they couldn't have kept him on past sixty-five, not really. 'Bureaucracy,' he'd spat, in disgust. But while he'd known it was coming, it was still a blow; one which she had somehow failed to protect him from. 'I'm useless,' he had said, more than once. It was no wonder he had died within the year. She had never been able to picture him an old man in any case.

There they were, Linda's smart bob swinging with every step, Daisy in her school hat trying to keep up and talking nineteen to the dozen. Sophia waved from the window, held up the teapot— but Linda pointed at her watch, kissed Daisy and turned away.

*   *   *

The day wore on. At six, cars heading out of the city on the bypass found a fine mist on their windscreens which made rubies of the tail lights ahead, and one by one they switched on their wipers. Rain sifted down, the last remnant of a shower that had discharged itself hours earlier over the Shropshire hills and which would, in under an hour, be nothing but a damp breeze. Now, though, it fell on the grimy pavements, the wheelie bins and pollarded street trees, on the grass of the little park and on the russet roof tiles of the house on Leasow Road. Daisy was back at home, crouching by the back door and ignoring both the drizzle on her arms and her mother's knocks on the kitchen window, because she was listening for her hedgehog.

Whether it had actually overwintered in the garden was a matter she had not yet determined. It would have been perfectly possible for her to have rooted through the grass cuttings piled up beside the shed—hot inside and ready to release thrilling curls of acrid smoke when the outer thatch was disturbed—or to have prodded the base of the pampas grass with a stick, but all winter she had felt protective of the garden's possibly imaginary hedgehog, and besides, it would have been unnecessarily dispiriting to have found nothing there. But now it was March, and mild, and the picture of the newly woken hedgehog shambling across the darkening lawn was so clear in Daisy's mind it was as though she had already seen it.

Behind her the back door opened, sticking slightly where the grey wood beneath the flaking white paint met the sill. A wedge of yellow light

100

spilled over the back step and reached across the rain-polished patio to where Daisy squatted, peering across the dark and sparkling lawn. 'Come on, darling, bedtime,' called Linda. Then the light sliced away as the door was pulled to.

'Bloody goddamn,' Daisy whispered experimentally. She sent a thought message to the hedgehog, apologising for not being able to wait; then, with a second brief squeal from the stiff door handle, she went inside, where the smell she brought in of wet earth faded even before the tiny rain-jewels disappeared from her hair.

Now the garden was returned, like all the gardens around, to the creatures to whom it really belonged. The sharp report of the back door's bolt being shot behind Daisy was noted not only by next door's cat, who soon came sidling yellow-eyed and evil-minded along the fence, but also by a hen blackbird who had reared three broods last year in a nest in the hydrangea and now roosted, gravid again, with her beady mate in next door's apple tree. They watched as the cat dropped soundlessly down the far side of the fence and slunk away, just as a tiny shadow detached itself from under the shed. It zigzagged between the blue-green spears of daffs and across the lawn to where a few fallen seeds and seed husks betrayed the hanging bird-feeder above. The wood mouse shared a nest of leaves and moss with several of its relatives in the shed's furthest corner, behind a tin of paint, and had nibbled the heads off the last of the crocuses, much to Linda's dismay. She had made a mental note to get the gardener to do something about it, before remembering she had cancelled him the week before. The reason for that was tied up, somehow, with her discovery of the bluebell wood, but she wasn't sure exactly how.

Before bed, Daisy fetched her pencil case and some paper and sat down at her homework table. She had been trying for two days to write to her grandmother, but so far it hadn't come out very well, and once more she had visited the old lady without the promised letter.

'*Dear Grandma, thank you for the seeds. How are you? I am very well,*' she had begun. Next, she would have liked to tell her all about what the hedgehog was doing, but given that she didn't know if he actually existed she thought it might count as a fib.

'*I have just been out in the garden looking for the hedgehog,*' she wrote instead. '*I didn't see him again and I don't know if he is even there. I couldn't wait very long because I had to go to bed even though I am not tired.*' Then she crossed it all out and sucked the end of her pen for a while.

Dear Grandma,
Thank you for the seeds. How are your daffodils?
I hope they are all jumbled up.
The hedgehog has woken up and we are best friends now. I am not going to give him a name because he is not a pet. He comes out when I go in the garden but not if anyone else is there, which is why only I have seen him. I found slugs for him to eat and I picked them up on a stick. He is very hungry because he has been asleep for a long time. But it is bad to give hedgehogs bread and milk because they might explode.
When you next come to visit me I will let you see him but you aren't allowed to tell anyone. Susie my friend hasn't seen him but that is

because he didn't know who she was not because he wasn't there. So I will tell him about you before you come over so that he knows you are nice.

It was turning out to be a very good letter after all. Daisy began to draw a hedgehog to fill up the rest of the page. She made him very spiky, and coloured him in brown, and she gave him a big smile. By the time she finished she could hear music and applause filtering up from the TV downstairs.

The rain faded away. As the darkness deepened, Daisy's house, and the rows of houses stretching out around it, became bright boxes of human concerns, leaving the gardens, the little park, the wooded common and the silent, faraway hills to their own mysterious imbroglios of fight, flight and survival. Wheeling over the furthest hills came Venus, while Orion hunted the sky to the south.

In the hawthorn hedge at the end of Daisy's garden the sparrows were finally still among the blossom, and deep in the motionless pampas a hedgehog scratched and sighed as it slept.

11

LADY DAY

A ceanothus outside Sophia's window produced three or four early, powder-blue blooms and was visited almost at once by a bee; Sophia, at her kitchen table, recorded its visit in her journal, where she had also just described, with enormous satisfaction, the daffodils, *'butter yellow or still in bud like sherbet twists'*, blooming outside her window for all the world as though they were wild.

It was Saturday morning, and she was looking after Daisy while Linda went to the shops; Steven was on a work deadline and Daisy wasn't very good at leaving him in peace. They had begun by working on their scrapbooks together, but when Daisy saw TC in the little park she had asked if she could go and play with him.

They had a conversation about the dangers—not just of strangers, and the busy road, but of snitching. 'It's only that your mummy worries, sweet pea,' Sophia said; the disloyalty, she told herself, had to stand against the benefits to Daisy of being trusted, and allowed to play for a bit without anyone telling her how. 'It's not a bad secret, I promise. Anyway, I'm still your mummy's mummy, and if I explain it to her properly she'll understand.'

'Hello!' Daisy yelled, outside, thundering up to TC.

'Hi.'

'Shall we play a game?'

'What game?'

'I don't know, any game. Are you still looking for the monster?'

'It wasn't a monster, it was a wolf.'

'Are you?'

'No.'

'Why not?'

TC was silent.

'Don't worry, it's probably hibernating. It'll wake up soon and then you can pretend again.'

TC got up and began walking off, Daisy doing hopscotch behind.

'Where are we going?'

'Come on.'

Where the path met the high road Daisy stopped.

'What's the matter?'

'I'm not allowed.'

'What?'

'Outside the park. I'm not allowed, not by myself.'

'Why not?'

Daisy shrugged. 'It's dangerous. You know.'

'Is it your nan won't let you?'

'No. Sort of. Where are you going?'

'Only to the common. It's just there.'

Daisy looked doubtful. 'Just a sec,' she said.

*　　　*　　　*

Sophia followed behind the two children, the *Reader's Digest* under her arm and half a packet of Viennese Whirls in her coat pocket. She was pleased with Daisy for asking, and pleased too to see her playing with the little boy. And a morning on the common was no bad thing. Last night had

105

been windy and wet, and the pavements were littered with sycamore tassels and twigs from which the sheath of bark was coming away like flesh around white bone. But now the sky was clean and cloud-chased, and the day was set fair.

Stepping carefully out onto Glebe Road she saw there were two crossed bones on the traffic island, grimy and talismanic. Fried chicken, said her rational brain, foxes. But the way they were placed was startling, a patteran for those with eyes to see. The world was full of mysteries, she reflected, cities no less so than anywhere else.

'Race you!' said TC when they got to the common.

'Don't go too far!' called Sophia after them, subsiding onto a bench with a crackle of biscuit packaging.

Daisy caught up with TC over by the oaks. 'See there,' he said, pointing to a hole at the base of one trunk.

'What?'

'Sometimes there are flowers there. Shop flowers.'

'Flowers? Why?'

'People put them there at night. Not a whole bunch, just a few. Nobody knows why.'

'That's stupid.'

'No it isn't.'

'What do they do it for, then?'

'I told you, nobody knows. Maybe the trees like it. Maybe for magic.'

Daisy giggled, but she could see that he was quite serious.

'Look!' she said then, pointing to the branch of an oak that was missing big patches of bark. Rusty

106

sap was bleeding from the wound, and there were scored marks, too, as though from teeth. 'What's done that?'

TC went to look, touching a careful finger to the sap. 'I don't know. Not squirrels.'

His face was troubled, and Daisy threw some leaves at his back. 'It's only a tree, it'll be all right. Anyway, there's loads. Come on!' she said, running off. TC followed, wondering whether the stripped bark was in his animal tracking book, and if somehow he had missed it.

'Those are its roots!' said Daisy, pointing at the huge root ball of the fallen tree. 'They used to be underground.'

'Come on then,' said TC, scrambling up. 'What—are you scared of getting dirty?'

'No!' Daisy retorted defiantly, but she could picture the look on her mother's face if she came back from her granny's with her clothes covered in mud.

'All right then,' said TC, sliding down, 'but you have to climb my tree.'

There were dog walkers and a few joggers on the path through the wood, so the two children lingered a little under the oaks. Finally the coast was clear, and TC boosted himself onto the lowest branch and scrambled up.

'Come on, it's easy!' he called, and so, gamely, and for the first time, Daisy began to climb.

The bark was damp and rough and made her hands sore, but it didn't matter. It was lovely; not scary at all. You had to think about it—which branch to get on next, and how—but that was all right. I'm super-strong, she thought, hauling herself up onto the same branch as TC and shuffling along to sit next to him. I bet I'm the strongest out of all my friends.

'Why is it your tree?' she asked.

TC shrugged. 'Just is. I've been coming here the longest. And nobody else climbs it except me.'

'And me, now.'

'Yeah, but only if I'm here. Not on your own.'

'I'm not allowed on my own anyway.'

'So do you—' TC stumbled slightly, looked down. 'D'you have lots of friends?'

'Oh, billions,' Daisy replied. 'My best friend is Susie though. She's got long hair.'

'Do you live with your mum and dad?'

'Yeah, course.'

'Have you got sisters and brothers?'

'No.' Daisy picked at a bit of skin on her hand that was coming off from the rough bark. 'I'm an only child. I'm not sad about it, though.'

'Why is it sad?'

'Oh, you know. Being lonely. But I'm not. Not mostly; not at school, anyway.'

TC thought about this, but it didn't seem to make any sense. What was he, then, if someone with a best friend and a mum and dad and a nan might be lonely?

'Are you rich?' he asked.

Daisy shrugged. 'Are you?'

'Do you go to the posh school?'

'What's the posh school?'

'The girls' one.'

'Oh. It's not posh, though. I think it's just normal.'

TC pictured the hats. They definitely weren't normal—or maybe they were if you were a different person. But if that was true, how did you ever know

108

how things really were? Who was right about the hats, in the end? The thought was weird, and he pushed it away.

'D'you want to be friends?' he asked instead.

'OK.'

'D'you want to play after school sometimes?'

But Daisy looked doubtful. 'My mummy—I'm always busy after school.'

'Doing your homework?'

'Sometimes. But other things—I do French and drama sometimes and I do ballet. What do you do?'

The trunk was warm and reassuring against his back. 'I come here,' TC replied.

From their perch they could see the path below, the train tracks, the football pitch and even the distant clay courts where a fat spaniel was cocking its leg on the one remaining net post. A lady with a pram passed below, and Daisy held her breath.

'We can see everything!' she whispered.

'And nobody can see us,' said TC. 'It's like we're birds, up here. Or squirrels.'

'Or secret spies!' she breathed. 'We can spy on everyone. We can collect evidence. We can find out about everything and have a secret code. Then, when they need evidence we'll show them everything we've collected and we'll be the best spies ever.'

'When who needs evidence?'

'You know . . .'

'The police?'

That wasn't right. Sometimes pretending was hard. 'No, the grown-ups. The grown-up spies who are rubbish.' By way of diversion she began whispering into her pink watch. 'Saturday morning,' she said, 'a man comes. He is tall and he has got a plastic bag.'

'That's stupid. Lots of people have plastic bags.'

'What then?'

'I know, let's go and look at his footprints!'

And so they spent the morning deep in covert operations, hatching plans in which Daisy would be crowned the cleverest and TC the most invisible—'the sneakiest,' Daisy said, meaning it kindly. A kind of shorthand developed between them, so that while what they were each picturing was not quite the same, it was close enough not to matter. They moved through a world in which the motives of adults were mysterious and suspect and their own superior skills went unrecognised, and little imagined how true it actually was.

*　　　*　　　*

Linda was on her way into town to do the department stores. She had decided to kit herself out with a good set of gardening tools. There were some in the shed, but they were mismatched and dirty, and if she was going to get into gardening it would be nice to have her own set. She was well aware that Steven would have gone to one of the big hardware centres, but it was much more fun to go into town.

She hadn't visited the local shops on the high road in years. There was nothing, absolutely nothing, there for her. It was grim: litter and pound shops and fast food and tacky clothing boutiques with sequinned polyester creations in the window, split to the thigh. The people who hung around there looked desperate or aggressive, even the children. Particularly the children.

110

Not only had she not shopped locally in years, she'd pretty much erased it from her mental image of where she lived. She rarely even drove along the high road, preferring to take a different route out of the area, one that led along the common, over the railway lines and then through some pretty Georgian squares. She took that route now, overtaking Denny, indicating left in his grimy van ('Dennis Webb: Clearances') and speeding past the white-painted bicycle that had recently appeared, chained to the railings near the station. Art project or something? she wondered. Probably.

She'd always loved shopping, ever since she was a little girl looking through catalogues, playing 'What would you choose on this page?' Back then there had not been the money for her to have what her mother called 'fancy' clothes, and even if there had been Sophia wouldn't have indulged Linda's wish for them; such things were frivolous, they weren't what was really important in life. Oh, but they were, they *were*; and Linda could still recall the shame of never having the right things, of always standing out at school. Nowadays she made sure that Daisy, at least, fitted in.

When she was a teenager it got worse; everything became a kind of code, everything somehow advertised your worth. For instance, the really smart girls at school had different make-up, not the kind that was advertised in *Jackie*, and their clothes were different, too. Where did they get them, and how did they know which were the right things to buy? It was years before she realised that it wasn't the clothes that were 'right', it was the girls, and that whatever they wore would have been invested with the same allure.

Now she lingered in the fragrance and skincare department, her practised eye skimming over the displays, looking for new product launches. She could still remember the first time she realised that someone normal—someone her own age and not famous or foreign—used posh toiletries, the kind you got from department stores rather than the local chemist. She was staying the night with a friend she had made at her first job, a chic girl called Patricia who was now, Linda was slightly aggrieved to recall, chief exec of an organic baby clothes company—or possibly baby food, she could never remember. They were both in their early twenties then, and seeing the expensive pots and bottles in the bathroom had made her look at Patricia with new eyes—yet when she finally dared to buy some too she was disappointed to find that, while it was nice enough to have, it refused to confer on her the same . . . what was it? Class?

There was a person Linda wanted to be, stylish and effortlessly confident; she could get within a hair's breadth, but the goalposts seemed always to shift slightly, and despite keeping up with the glossy magazines she could never quite get it right. Nevertheless, every trip to the shops was another chance to transform herself once and for all, and more immediately an opportunity to exercise her ability to choose. It was good to know which things *not* to buy, at least, and to understand the nuances of price and brand and positioning; it was good to play the game as well as you could. The alternative was invisibility.

Linda rose smoothly up through the atrium in a glass lift. The gardening section, when she found it, wasn't huge, but the things in it spoke to her in a way that the racks of tools in a DIY hangar never would have. She chose a canvas trug full of 'heritage' hand tools with lathe-turned ash handles, a pair of floral gardening gloves, a wooden dibber and a set of copper plant labels, and arranged for a matching ash-handled border spade and fork and six distressed terracotta pots to be delivered to the house.

At home she took her purchases out to the shed. The tools that were already there looked reproachful and untidy, and she stacked them in one corner, making room for her new spade and fork when they arrived. She set the trug on the shelf; dusty sunlight filtered through the Perspex panes and lent it a look of something that had always been there. The floral gloves, though, looked brash, and she could see they would have to go back.

'Glass of wine?' she called to Steven as she went back into the house. He emerged from the study with the dazed, close-focused air of someone who had been staring at a screen for far too long. 'Go on then,' he said. 'I'm about finished for the day, anyway.'

'What is it?'

'A bottle—you know, the sports type, to fit on a bike. Needs to have hand grips, but space for the fixings, too.'

'Tricky.'

'Not really . . . it shouldn't be. I just hate working on weekends.'

'I know.' She handed him a glass. 'Oh, wait—hadn't one of us better collect Daisy first?'

'Don't worry, your mum's going to drop her back.'

'Really? When?'

'Oh . . . sometime before supper.'

Linda put her glass down and turned away. 'Well, I can't start making it, then.'

'Why not?'

'Because, Steve, she'll see I'm cooking and she'll want to stay.'

'No she won't. And anyway, is that so bad?'

'Of course not, but you know I like to know. In advance, so I'm ready. And I wouldn't have opened the wine.'

'I'd've thought that would help,' said Steven, smiling; but he could see from the set of her shoulders that it wasn't going to be as easy as all that.

*   *   *

Daisy and TC were walking back from the common behind Sophia. Daisy had had a lovely time; one of her best times ever, probably. She thought about what TC had said, but she knew she wouldn't be allowed to play after school, not unless it was all arranged. And although she couldn't have said why, she didn't think, somehow, that the arranging would be able to happen.

'What do you want to be when you grow up?' she asked, skipping a bit as they went. 'I'm going to be a spy, or famous. Or do parties, like my mum.'

TC shrugged.

'Come on, you must want to be something. Is it a footballer?'

'No.'

'What then?'

'I don't know.'

'Yes you do,' she said, nudging him a little. 'Go on, say!'

'I *told* you, I don't know,' he muttered, something in his voice making Sophia look round.

'Give over, Daisy,' she said. 'He doesn't have to decide now.'

'He could be a spy, too; I don't mind. Or a soldier.'

'*Daisy!*'

'But I'm not even doing anything!'

It was too late. 'I've got to go,' TC said. 'Bye, Daisy. Bye, Mrs . . .'

'Sophia,' Sophia supplied, as the boy slipped through the traffic on Litten Close and away.

'He doesn't want to be *anything*,' Daisy pronounced conclusively. 'Come on. Are you having supper at our house tonight?'

*   *   *

When Jozef got to the cafe he saw that the boy was already there. He was at the same table they'd sat at last time, the one by the window, which he held, eyes wide, looking very young among the garrulous Polish crowd. He looked relieved when Jozef arrived.

Znajda grinned indiscriminately at people's legs and feet as they edged through the tables. She greeted TC enthusiastically, pushing her nose at him and wagging her tail ecstatically before subsiding with a thump onto her side and presenting her ribs for a scratch. Jozef liked the way she was with TC, and could see the confidence the boy took from being around the dog, how pleased he was that she recognised him each time. It was

115

such a small thing to give the boy, and he wondered how little there must be in TC's life that it would show.

'You hungry?'

TC nodded.

'OK.' Jozef hung his jacket on the back of the chair and put his holdall on the seat, then made his way to the counter. While he waited to order he looked over at the boy and saw Znajda wag the stump of her tail at Agata, the waitress; she had once dropped a half-eaten blood sausage, only partly by mistake. Jozef was her favourite customer; he was polite to her, for one thing, and unlike many of the other regulars he had not tried to sleep with her.

'Food is coming,' Jozef said to TC, taking his seat. 'First we eat, then we play. You remember how?'

'Yeah,' said TC.

'OK, good. Because this is serious now. Man to man, OK?'

TC grinned and drank his Coke.

'You want to know why it is so serious?'

'Why?'

'I show you. So. Today we don't play with the usual pieces, OK?' He slid a cardboard box from the plastic bag and placed it reverently on the table. 'Today, we play with a new set.' He turned the box to face TC, opening the lid and watching the boy's face.

TC reached in and took out a lynx, and then a hare.

'They're all animals.'

'Yes.'

'You made them.'

116

'Yes, I made them.'

'Are they wood?'

'Yes.'

'How did you do it?'

'With a knife—my father's knife. He taught me. Is not easy—see these scars? And here?—but I have been doing it for a very long time.'

'How long?'

'Since I was your age.'

'Will you teach me?'

Jozef considered the boy. 'What do you think your mother would say?'

'My . . . ? She won't mind.'

'Does she know you are here, even?'

TC put the animals down and looked past Jozef to the street outside. 'Spect so.'

Jozef sighed.

'Look, mister, you don't have to teach me. I don't care.'

'TC, it is a different thing to have a knife here, in the city, than for a small Polish farm boy, OK?'

TC looked at his lap. 'I'm not gonna do anything stupid.'

'I know that.'

'Well then.'

Jozef regarded him for a long moment. 'I will think about it. OK? So. What have you been doing this week?'

'Not much.'

'School OK?'

'Yeah.'

'You know, when I was a boy I often did not go to school.'

'Why not?'

'My father was a farmer. He needed me.'

117

'What, so he let you stay off school?'

'Yes, sometimes. But for work. Not for fun. And it was hard work, believe me.'

'Is your dad dead now?'

Jozef looked out of the window at the row of backs leaning up against the Perspex bus shelter outside. 'Yes. But what I am telling you is he shouldn't have taken me out of school. Because if I'd had more lessons, maybe I would still have the farm today. Who knows.'

'Why, what happened to your farm?'

'The future came. And I was not ready for it.'

'What do you mean? Because you hadn't done your exams?'

'We had to make big changes, for the EU. You know the EU? Well—don't worry. But I didn't want to learn the new ways. I wanted to do the same ways as my father, and his father. So. And when I had to change, I made mistakes, I get it wrong. I lost my farm.'

TC looked down at his lap. 'But I don't like school.'

'I can see.'

'I do go, more than I used to. I nearly always go.'

'And other times?'

TC shrugged. 'I got stuff to do.'

Jozef looked at the boy for a long moment. He was far from the only child missing lessons in the area, but the kids who hung around the park benches and the newsagent in the afternoon were loud and streetwise, and couldn't have been more different from TC's fathomless reticence and shy regard. It was as though he lived in a different world altogether from the one inhabited by his peers.

118

'This stuff—it is more important than school?'

'Yeah.'

'Does your mother know?'

'She doesn't care.'

'But does she know?'

'I don't know, all right? *Fuck.*'

Jozef could see the boy was near tears. 'OK, *moje dziecko*, OK. It is not my business. I would like it if you would go to school, that is all.'

'Why?'

Jozef shrugged. 'I think you are a smart kid. Other kids around here, some of them—' he made a gesture like throwing something away—'they will do nothing all their lives. But you . . . you are different, I think. School is hard—OK. And even harder if you are . . . different. But the things you learn now, they help you learn other things in the future. And some of *those* things, I promise you, you will like. Then you can choose your life, because of what you do now. OK?'

TC looked down and said nothing. Jozef took out the king and queen and stood them carefully next to each other on the table, then leaned back and folded his arms. The boy picked them up slowly and examined them, turning the shapes carefully in his hands.

'This one's Znajda,' he said, his voice soft.

'Yes.'

'And this one's a wolf.'

'Yes. The king. He is howling, you see. Do you like him?'

'He's brilliant.' The boy's eyes shone. 'Can I set the board up?'

'In a moment,' Jozef replied. 'Food is coming, look.'

   *   *   *

After they had eaten TC got up to go to the toilet and Agata came and sat in his chair.

'I didn't know you had a son,' she said, in Polish.

'He's not my son,' Jozef replied. 'He's—a friend.'

'A friend? What is he, seven, eight? You were here with him once before, right?'

'He's nine. Nearly ten.'

'Somebody you know's child?'

'We just . . . I met him in the park, one night—' She raised one eyebrow. 'Don't be silly, Agata. He doesn't really have anyone, and he's a good kid. I like him.'

'His mother knows where he is?'

'Of course.'

'Good. Because you're not in the village now, Jozef. A single man, in his forties—people can be suspicious here.'

TC returned and stood uncertainly by the table. As she left with their plates Agata shot Jozef a look over his head. 'Be careful,' it said. Jozef looked away.

12

HOCK TIDE

The girls racketed out of the coach and into the car park, Miss Carter counting straw hats while Mr Baker waved them into a rough assembly. The coach's engine wheezed and shuddered and was quiet, the driver climbing out of the opposite side and making for the facilities. Miss Carter began handing out pencils and paper; the girls were already in pairs from the coach, sticky hands held and only a little bickering.

Up the track was a chalk hillside prospected by children from six local schools for generations, barely a stem unmapped, yet each class pioneering it anew. The children had transects measuring a foot square, magnifying glasses and a laminated sheet showing all the plant species each pair was likely to find, and their job was to count the different kinds. The really sensitive habitat was further away, fenced off to protect it from trampling by hordes of children's feet.

From the very top of the hill only a smudge on the horizon bore witness to the distant city fomenting beneath it. Occasionally the slopes gave up little whorled shells, impossibly old, that were lost in the grass or crushed to fragments of sand under walkers' feet, while deep in its wooded lower slopes dank pillboxes and crumbling gun emplacements spoke of a less bucolic past.

Once at the site the children sat down cross-legged while Miss Carter ran through their task for the last time. Settling down beside Daisy, Susannah's eyes grew wide.

'Daisy!' she hissed, nudging her furiously. 'Daisy!'

'What?'

'You picked a flower!' And it was true; tucked behind Daisy's ear was a pink betony spire in full bloom.

'So?'

'We're not supposed to! Miss Carter said! It might be rare!'

'It's not,' replied Daisy. 'I can see hundreds.'

'Throw it away! Throw it away!'

'But I've picked it now. I might as well keep it, hadn't I?'

'Oh . . .' In her agitation, Susannah was as close to wringing her hands as an eight-year-old can be. 'Please, Daisy! Daisy! *Pleeease!*'

'Oh, all right. But I'm not throwing it away.' Daisy took the flower from her hair and slipped it into the pocket of her school dress.

'Daisy! Susannah! No talking please!' called Mr Baker. The rest of the class looked over. Daisy grinned back, while Susannah looked down at their illustrated card, her hair falling around her face. After a long moment, Miss Carter continued, holding up the card and pointing out the different flowers and grasses on it.

'I'm hungry,' whispered Daisy, nudging Susannah in the ribs. 'What have you got for lunch?'

Susannah didn't answer.

'Susie!' Daisy's whisper threatened to grow louder, and Susannah threw her a desperate sidelong glance. Their lunches were in the coach; it wasn't as though they could have them now anyway.

'I bet you've got cheese strings,' muttered Daisy accusingly, kicking a little at Susannah's foot just in case. She was not—would never be—allowed anything as garish or convenient as cheese strings, and as a result found them impossibly alluring. Their households were quite different, in ways that both of them understood, could not have described and attached no value to. Daisy no more questioned the fact that Susie didn't go to Little Thesps or La Jolie Ronde French or Art Attack than she wondered why her own mother did not collect china animals. It was just the way the world was, and was no more mysterious than anything else.

During lunch break Daisy and Susannah made daisy chains, Daisy's longer but Susannah's more neatly strung. They gave them to Miss Carter, who smiled and draped them carefully around her wrist. Despite the profusion of flowers they looked somehow limp and defeated.

The afternoon's activities were all about invertebrates. Mr Baker spread a white sheet under a tree and reached up to shake the branches. Some of the girls squealed to see the earwigs and crab spiders and other insects drop down, but Daisy and Susannah knelt on the edge of the sheet and brushed them carefully into little pots with paint brushes. The pots had special lids that let you see them up close, and Mr Baker had a laptop with a plug-in microscope for anything really tiny or really interesting. Some of them looked quite fearsome until you remembered how small they really were.

Daisy had decided she was going to find a stag beetle. There was a picture of one on their insect sheet, and it was the biggest thing by miles. It obviously wasn't going to fall out of an oak tree, so she headed away from the group to poke around the tree boles. She hummed slightly to herself, and thought about building a house for a stag beetle. What would it need? Would it be underground? She decided on more of a cabin-style arrangement, partly because the handout said they liked wood and partly because it would be more fun to make. All it would take was some good bits of bark, and maybe some stones to make a front garden. And a stag beetle, of course; though if she couldn't find one she could always make the house anyway, and one might move in after they had gone. Perhaps Susie could help. But no, Susie would want to follow the instructions, and anyway if she did find a stag beetle it would be nicer to have done it all by herself.

She tried to imagine what Miss Carter would say. She would be very pleased, of course, and would probably ask her to show the beetle to the whole class and describe how she found it. Afterwards Daisy would show it its new home. It would love it and would go straight in and it would probably live there forever.

It didn't take long for Daisy to be missed. Susannah looked around for her and she wasn't there. She didn't say anything straight away, as Daisy would be very cross if she got her in trouble when she was really quite nearby. But she wasn't anywhere. Susannah felt her eyes go hot and her throat tight. She went to find Miss Carter.

*　　　*　　　*

In the city the day was warming up. In the past

week spring had fallen like a benediction, the sun warming the grimy pavements, charming weed shoots through the cracks and drawing blind thistles up under the tarmac in unlikely bulges. The grass had begun to grow, re-greening the gardens, the parks and the verges with their cargos of litter and cuckoo spit and grime. Even the waste ground between the old bingo hall and the railway line, strewn with faded estate agents' boards, rotting sleepers and huge wooden drums once wound with cable, even these abandoned corners were warmed by the spring sunshine and had become rank and dizzy with life.

On Leasow Road the cherries blushed cornelian or dappled the pavement below with palest pink. Outside some lucky houses magnolias were opening their miraculous, waxy blooms, their fallen petals like slivers of soap on the pavements beneath, bruising to brown with time, and feet. On earthy islets in crazy-paved front gardens specimen roses unfurled new, red leaves, while from verge, bed and central reservation nodded the municipal daffs.

Now the Somali postman found himself shadowed on his rounds by wood pigeons' dozy coos, while on sunny afternoons starlings clicked and chattered from the aerials like avian telegraph operators sending news about each street's coming and goings on the wires. And along the long, unlovely high road the estates were once again jubilant with birds. Robins sang riotously from street lamp, sill and gutter; blackbirds spilled their song down into the tangled yards behind the high-rise blocks. Pigeons jostled the windowsills above grimy shopfronts, and at sunset their assemblies were hosted by the sun-warmed roofs.

125

The spring sunshine brought a new mood of optimism everywhere it fell. Workmen left doors and windows open, causing all but the most stubbornly unmusical to fall into step with their radios as they passed. Women, bound by the same circadian rhythm, swapped gloves for sunglasses in their everyday handbags. And at the end of each school day the kids streamed screaming out of the gates, eager not for home and TV, but just to be out, free, in the burgeoning world.

TC, his school sweatshirt stuffed into his backpack, was sidling along an alley off Curtilage Street. It smelled of urine and was full of wind-blown litter, but the fence on one side was starred with ivy leaves pushing through the slats from the other side, evidence of a press of vegetation beyond. He was exploring: looking for tangly areas, odd corners of waste ground, places where foxes might be bringing up cubs. Along the railway track was a good place; the line was a highway for animals in and out of the city, as well as people.

Scaling the fence with the help of a wheelie bin, he dropped down on the other side, almost disappearing into the long grass and vetch beneath. A hen blackbird took off into the trees, clucking and bubbling into a loud 'ack-ack-ack!' of alarm.

It was a forgotten half-acre, fenced off, overgrown and utterly abandoned. The large, detached house that had once stood there had fallen victim to a V-1 over half a century before and had been demolished. Its foundations had been colonised first by the rosebay willowherb that wreathed the mourning city in the wake of war, then by the pragmatic buddleia, and were now so blanketed in brambles and ivy that it was hard to see where the house had ever stood. After the war the land had been willed to a relative, an Australian who had little interest in a city plot half a world away, and whose daughter, who now owned the deeds, even less so. And so instead of being buried underneath a new block of flats, or paved for parking, the garden persisted: kingcups marked the boggy place where once there was a pond; there were three stunted rhododendrons amid the brambles; and almost lost among the lime and sycamore saplings were two rusty sequoias and a larch, nearly 120 foot high, survivors of the garden's Victorian apogee.

What was immediately clear to TC was that nobody went there—nobody at all. No dogs, no teenagers, no wastermen with their beer cans and ganja. It was a lost world, and it belonged to him. He closed his eyes for a moment to take it in.

The next thing he did was walk the bounds of his new kingdom, just to understand its dimensions. For much of the way he had to fight through nettles and sticky goosegrass and whippy bramble stolons. That meant blackberries later in the year, which was good.

He decided to find out every single thing that lived there, so he could take care of it all. Already he'd seen blackbirds and robins and squirrels skittering crabwise up the trunks of trees, and he could hear a woodpecker drumming.

At the back of the garden there was a pollard oak that predated even the garden, all tortuous elbows above a short trunk. Its shape was proof that the land had once been grazed, the tree pruned so that it would produce new branches at a height safe from the reach of inquisitive livestock. But the grazing land had been swallowed up by the expanding city, and the oak became part of a grand garden, for a while. Now, unobserved and long unpollarded, it was abandoned to time.

The brambles gave way to ivy and nettles beneath the oak's canopy, and around the trunk itself the ground was clear. TC leaned against it and rested his cheek on the rough, cool bark. A leaf-green caterpillar dangled on an invisible thread, its gently twisting body lit by the sundazzle filtering through the tessellating leaves above. TC knew about oak trees: more things lived in them than any other kind of tree. Here, against its protective trunk, was where he would have his hide.

On TV hides were things like sheds with slits to look through, or tents covered in camouflage netting. His would be better, because it would be made of sticks, which were natural. There were lots of branches around, but he had to tear most of them free from the ivy, and some were rotten and crumbled away in his hands. Under them worms eased away into the loam and woodlice and pale orange centipedes slipped quickly into the leaf litter. The exposed earth smelled richly of decay.

TC began to see that there were things hidden in the ivy: roof slates, a coil of rusted wire, a grey, flattened bucket, the footing for a wall. It wasn't litter or fly-tipping; he could tell it had all been here for ages, and was part of the place, somehow. It made him have a quiet feeling that he didn't completely understand. In fact, although he could not have known it, as he explored the uneven ground he was moving through the ghostly rooms of the long-gone house: kitchen, scullery, drawing

128

room, hall. How strange the house's last inhabitants would have found the little boy; or, perhaps, not so very strange at all.

He found a lumpen accretion of bricks and concrete half hidden by a clump of honesty in full bloom, a little path snaking between the stems and leading deep beneath the stony mass. Carefully, he put his eye to it. No cobwebs, no leaves. It must be in use. Did snakes live in holes? Probably, but TC decided it was more likely to belong to a mouse. He wished he had some bread; he could have made tiny dough balls and rolled them into the hole for it to eat. Next time.

He wondered how far the tunnel went, and what was at the end of it. He imagined a cosy burrow packed with happy, well-fed baby mice and snug with warm fur and breath. If only he could have lifted the concrete mass to see, and replaced it gently without waking them; if only he could prove he meant no harm.

It was a warm afternoon, but the secret garden was sun-dappled and cool. Between the shafts of sunlight hoverflies hung, moved and hung still again, piloted like tiny futuristic airships.

Time slowed, and the task at hand filled TC's mind. Simply to apprehend the sticks and the ivy and the simple truths of the living things around him was enough, and he let his mind go out to it in quietness. His mother's silences and sharp eye, and the empty flat that he would later go home to, these things all left him, and, as precise and intent as a blackbird turning leaf litter, he became a part of the garden. He had no way of knowing that the world he longed to secede from would one day run him to ground there; for now, he only knew himself to

129

be ten years old and beyond the ken of any living human being.

*   *   *

That day the sycamores on the common unfurled their acid-green leaves all at once. Along with the oaks and the lone ash they were slow each year to come into leaf. The big horse chestnut beside the church was not only fully clothed, but in flower.

Linda had downloaded an app for her phone about trees. A few she remembered from childhood; some she was half familiar with, like people you see at work but don't know, so that putting a name to them was like being introduced. Yet her dad must have taught her all of them, and she wondered when it was she had stopped taking an interest, and why. Being curious about plants and trees and things seemed more or less unthinking for Daisy, and her mother was like that even now, looking at things, wondering about them. Why, then, had she stopped?

It was good to be the one to tell Daisy things, too, although you had to pick your moment. There were times when all she was interested in talking about was Olivia's hair, or Jack's party, or whichever cartoon series she was currently obsessed with. Get the timing right, though, and she felt as her father must have felt, teaching her. True, his knowledge wasn't from an app, it was a lot more deep-rooted than that, but still, she was trying. The other day, for instance, she had spotted a plane tree on the way in to school, and had pointed out the way its bark flaked off in patches. When Daisy had asked why, she had been able to tell her: the

130

bark fell off when it got pollution on it, so that the tree could breathe. The leaves trapped pollution too, which was why people planted plane trees in cities: they helped keep the air clean. Telling her had been a little triumph. Steven had laughed when Linda had told him about it later, but kindly.

Steven was working on site and couldn't get away, so Linda had come back from work a little early so as to be home when Daisy returned from her school trip. Perhaps Daisy could help her make supper, if she could think of something fun to make; she probably wouldn't have homework after a field trip.

At that age, she and Michael would have gone out on their bikes until their tea was ready, their empire the little park, the common, the sweet shop and all their friends' houses and back gardens; but the only time you saw children on Leasow Road was as they got into, or out of, cars for the school run. There were children on their road the same age as Daisy whom Daisy had never met.

When Linda answered the doorbell, Miss Carter was there with Daisy, whose cheeks were pink and bore a suspicion of dried tears but who also wore an obdurate expression Linda knew well. Raising her eyebrows, she ushered them both in.

'I can't stop, Mrs Collis,' said the teacher.

Linda caught hold of Daisy as she tried to march past, turning her round and holding her shoulders.

'We had a bit of an . . . incident on the field trip today. Daisy wandered off on her own. It wasn't for long, and she came when she heard us calling, but it's very important she understands that she can't just go off and play by herself.'

'No, of course. I'm so sorry she worried you.

131

Daisy, what on earth were you doing?'

'Nothing! I didn't even go anywhere!' Daisy folded her arms, but her cheeks grew red.

'Daisy. What do you say?'

'I already have.'

'I beg your pardon, young lady?'

'Sorry, Miss Carter.' Daisy twisted in her mother's grip. 'Can I go upstairs now?'

'Yes. Off you go. And wash your hands.'

As Daisy disappeared to her room with a clatter, Linda's brow furrowed.

'Bryony—Miss Carter. Can I ask how long it was before my daughter's absence was noticed?'

Miss Carter coloured a little. 'Just minutes, Mrs Collis. Susannah raised the alarm. We'll have to put in a report, unfortunately. We have to keep records of this sort of thing now.'

'Good. I'd like to see a copy. Thank you for bringing her back.' And with that, the two women smiled briefly at each other, and the heavy door swung closed.

*   *   *

'*Dear Grandma, today I am very cross,*' Daisy wrote. She was using a red felt tip and pressing hard, and had not yet washed her hands. '*Susie ran away and got lost and nobody knew where she was. It was on a school trip. I told her not to but she went to play by herself like at your house but without asking. Now she is in trouble but it isn't fair because she didn't do anything.*' The felt tip's nib had got a bit spread out, so she changed it for a biro.

'*I haven't started our flower bed project yet because I am very busy but I will on Saturday. I am sending*

132

you a flower. I don't know what it is because I forgot to look it up and then we had to give in our charts. I hope you like it. Love, Daisy.'

The betony was limp from being in her pocket all day and some of its petals had come off. She folded the sheet of paper in half, the betony inside, and pressed it all down very flat.

*   *   *

Clouds of midges danced about TC's head as he scaled the fence and headed back up Curtilage Street. Half past seven: the sky was still light but the rays of the sun had gone, and with them the day's warmth.

A faint *tseep*ing filtered down to him from high in the house eaves, evidence of baby sparrows in the guttering. There would be nests in the secret garden, too; there had to be. Maybe he could sit in a tree and watch the eggs hatch.

The signs on the high road were bright and indecipherable: Billa's Foneshop, Ca$h Money Transfer, Top Joe, International Nails. He passed them with his head down, feeling in his pocket for some money. Nuggets maybe. If he had two pounds.

On Leasow Road the verges were crowded with daisies shut fast against the dusk. Bins night: the pavements were an obstacle course of recycling crates and sacks. TC dribbled an imaginary football past Daisy's house, scoring with a silent cheer between the two bottle banks at the end of the street.

133

13

MAY DAY

In the little park the spring mornings did not come dramatically, with birds that proclaimed the new day from the rooftops. Rather, a robin let loose a low undersong, as it had from time to time throughout the night; but this time it kept singing, half to itself, half to anyone else who cared to listen. High and sweet and plaintive, the notes trickled down from the lone ash to the darkened pavements and the hushed grass. The orange street lights hummed obliviously, and a rat hugged the shadow of the wall beside the road. Then, from one of the horse chestnuts, threshed in green, came an answering note. The robin cocked its head to one side, summoned its voice, and replied.

As the sky began slowly to lighten the birds who roosted in the park began to give song. Most strident were the wrens, more numerous than nearly anybody knew, their tiny nut-brown bodies haunting the undergrowth up to a man's height. The blackbird's song was a tumble, a roundy well-made torrent that proclaimed through its variety the extent of its author's travels, and so his fitness as a suitor and as a rival.

As the sky grew pale the sparrows began to gossip and quarrel in the ivy behind the benches, their insistent chirruping giving them away, and from his favourite perch high in the little rowan came the mistle thrush's fluting song. He had survived his second winter largely due to a firethorn planted by the council against the wall of one of the blocks in the estate, feasting on its berries for nearly a month in late autumn and defending it against all comers. As spring wore on his rattling alarm call announced the arrival of each pedestrian and dog walker in the little park.

The sky slowly became blue, the piercing 'Teacher! Teacher!' of the great tits and the 'tseep, tseep' of the blue tits cutting through the rumble of the early buses. In the brambles which carpeted the furthest corner of the park a chiffchaff sang his own name over and over. A diffidently dressed harbinger of summer, he was not long in from Spain and scouting for territory. Country-dwelling nature columnists noted their arrival in the broadsheets, but few people, Sophia excepted, would have guessed that the small city park had its own pair.

And so the day began with birds, and with the night-time creatures going to bed. A dog fox trotted silently out of the park onto Leasow Road to kennel under a shed for the day, just as the first early shift workers crossed the grass to the bus stop. His belly was full of chicken bones and baby rats and squabs, for it had been a good night's work. The rats whose nest he had robbed had run from him into a drain in the road, but it would only be a month before they would have another litter. The baby pigeons were nestfall, already cold.

*   *   *

TC had been up and about since dawn. He'd found his mum asleep on the sofa when he got up, the room close and stale, the ashtray on the carpet full of spliff butts, and had crept out without waking

135

her.

He had done the rounds of the common and now cut through the little park, making for Curtilage Street and the secret garden. He had half an hour before he had to be at school. He crossed the grass in front of Sophia's kitchen window, giving the Jamaican man a wide berth where he stood shouting at the cars. Poor lost, lonely boy, Sophia thought, as she watched him pass. Why don't his parents do something?

Jamal had not been to the flat for ages, and TC knew that it was over between him and his mother. He wondered what he felt about it, but found he couldn't tell. It wasn't like when his dad left; it didn't change anything much. It wasn't like Jamal was in his family.

What was that, anyway—family? The three of them, he supposed: him, his mum and his dad. When they all lived together, when they used to do things together. He thought about Christmas Day, and watching telly together. What else?

You didn't have to be related, though; you could be adopted and that would be family, if you said it was, if everyone wanted it to be. Someone who looked after you—that could be family. Who got you toys and clothes, made sure you had your dinner. Jamal did that—he'd tried to, anyway—but he wasn't family; Jozef, too, and he was practically a stranger. And his mum didn't, not much, but she *was* family, they were a family by themselves now. Weren't they?

She was hardly in any more, anyway. She had got a job at the bookies and sometimes didn't finish until gone ten o'clock. He got himself something to eat in the evenings, usually: beans on toast, spaghetti hoops, hot dogs, microwave cottage pie. At least now there were two pound coins on the kitchen table for him most weekday mornings— although not today.

He humped his school bag further up his back and turned into Curtilage Street. Ten minutes, that was all he wanted. Just to have a look. It was a showery morning, but a brisk breeze moved the weather on quickly enough and between times the sun was warm.

In the secret garden the undergrowth was damp and the air smelled green. TC dropped from the fence like a stone into a still pool and crouched in the long grass, listening. Minutes passed, and the sun-dappled garden closed around him until he was part of it.

*　　　*　　　*

At noon Sophia emerged from the flats and made for the benches. The desire paths had done brief duty as watercourses in the dark, and testified to it now with little cargos of flotsam caught against the tree roots here and there. Pale sand, light and easiest borne, showed where the fastest runnels had been.

She held the back of the bench with her free hand and looked up. It was hard to balance, even with her stick, but in the city you had to look up if you wanted to see a good bit of sky. Nothing yet, she thought, though it's hardly the day for them. And it might be my eyes. She was waiting for the first swifts to appear, their sickle shapes scything the blue and proving that summer had really arrived. Outside the city there'd been swallows and house martins three weeks ago and more, but they weren't so often to be seen this far into the city; swifts, though, flew in high above the pollution, quartering schools of aerial plankton like sleek little basking sharks. They built their wattle-and-daub nests high on the city's churches, offices and multi-storeys, the raising of young being their only reason for landing at all. Nesting was a temporary concession to gravity; if they could have raised their chicks on the wing, they would.

Yesterday would have been a good day for them, Sophia thought, the air still, the gardens full of greenflies wafting up from the city on thermals. All the way from Africa for some insects: it was amazing. But perhaps they were here already, and she had missed them. Once their screams would have been enough to have given them away, but she had lost that register several years ago.

Always this anxiousness to know if they had made it. A sign that the world was still working, despite everything. A tiny reassurance in her old age.

*   *   *

A handbell sounded the end of lunch hour at the private school, its lazy notes drifting into back gardens two streets away. Slowly the sun burned off the last of the cloud and the afternoon settled into full-blown and blowsy warmth. The ground in the little park was warm and full of weed seeds secretly germinating, and the grass there and on the common was thick and lush.

Jozef found he loved the spring afternoons. To walk Znajda in the warm, golden light was to pass from one blackbird's demesne into another's, their songs a carillon calling him down the peaceful streets. May blossom clotted the hawthorns by the high road, and here and there wisteria hung in opulent watercolour from the house-fronts. The smell of lilacs and cut privet hung over the pavements and produced in him the same strange intensity of feeling as déjà vu.

He thought about the city, how ordinary and beautiful it was, and wondered if he would think the same had he been born there. Yet he missed Poland, too; not just his farm, but the way he could make sense of it, because he was born into its stories and its history. In his village you could trace the shape of the past: here was once the ford, before the road bridge was built, here the mill; this was once the old road to the next village. Perhaps the city streets he walked with Znajda told stories, too, but he had not yet learned how to decipher them.

There was an ancient pollard ash that had once marked the westernmost boundary of his farm. His father, and his father's father, and his great-grandfather, back and back—all of them must have known it. When Jozef had last seen it, it had been more or less absorbed into the old hazel coppice behind it, but at one time it had stood alone along a cart track flanked by a boundary ditch dug by who could say which of his forebears. For a long time that track was one of the three roads out of the village, and the tree had stood at a slight bend and marked the furthest point at which generations of villagers could turn and wave, when leaving the village for the market, or for Kraków, or for war, before being lost from sight. In his own time the

139

track had fallen into disuse and the ash tree no longer had a place in the life of the village, but he had held the knowledge in himself, given to him by his father, along with a thousand other things about the land he had been born on and had farmed, the very last in his line. Jozef wondered if the tree still stood, or had been grubbed up, the coppice razed for rows of ugly metal pig sheds. He pushed his hands into his pockets and picked up his pace.

Jozef took a left before reaching the high road. Eventually Denny would hear of Znajda's return, and then they would have to have a talk, but until then Jozef would not walk her too close to the shop. 'You gonna keep her, get her fix,' Musa had said. 'That way she no good to Denny any more.' Jozef's first instinct had been to reject out of hand a plan to cause the dog further harm, but in his private moments he could see there was sense in it. He was putting his money by for his own place, but once that was done, perhaps.

*   *   *

He waited for TC at the school gate, standing diffidently across the road, away from all the mothers and their disapproving gaze. He'd grown used to people crossing the road at the sight of Znajda, or flinching when she sniffed their passing legs, but while it still pained him from time to time to see her so badly judged he had to admit that outside a primary school was not the best place to put people's prejudices to the test.

TC was one of the last children to emerge, and Jozef had begun to think that perhaps he hadn't been to school that day. But then there he was, struggling with the straps of his backpack behind a group of kids who took off, shouting and cat-calling to one another, towards the high road. Jozef waved him over and took his bag from him as the boy knelt down and greeted Znajda.

'I was coming this way,' Jozef said, 'and Znajda, she wanted to see you. It is OK?'

'Yeah,' replied TC, and grinned.

'Where you going? You going home?'

TC shook his head.

'Good, then we take her for a walk.'

The afternoon light lay long and golden on the common, the shadows of the trees reaching out across the grass. As they came off the path Znajda took off for the sheer joy of it, tearing around in wide circles and sending pigeons exploding like skeet out of the thickets. When Jozef whistled her back she thundered to his feet and collapsed, pushing her ears against the ground and rolling shamelessly on her back.

'*Głupi pies, Znajda,*' he laughed, nudging her with his foot. 'Get up, stupid dog.'

They walked on. 'So you were at school today,' said Jozef.

'Yeah.'

'That's good. All day?'

'Nearly all. I do go, you know. I said I went.'

'I know, I know. Was it OK?'

TC shrugged.

'Do you have—do you have friends?'

'Not really. They're all stupid.'

'Is there nobody you play with?'

'I played with that girl Daisy the other day, you know, on the common, but she goes to a different school.' TC looked up. 'Can we get chips?' he

141

asked, colouring slightly. 'Only, I didn't have lunch today. I was . . . I wasn't hungry.'

'Of course. We will walk that way. So. Tell me what you usually do after school—you go and play on the common . . . what else?'

'Homework.'

'Ah, homework. That's good. You do that at home, though, yes?'

'Yeah. Watch TV sometimes. Why?'

'But you prefer to be outside.'

'Yeah. It's . . . it's . . .'

'Where the important things are? I was the same, you know, when I was young. And now, also, I still feel like that.'

Now it was TC's turn to ask. 'Do you miss your farm, then?'

'All the time. When you know some land—properly, you know, really know it—is like . . . is like it never leaves you.'

TC was nodding sagely. 'I know the whole common—and lots around here. I know everything, nobody knows the things I know.'

'I believe you.'

'I've—I've got a secret place, an old garden. You can't tell anyone. Nobody goes there except me, no one even knows about it, not even the council.'

Jozef had a brief vision of the abandoned farm three *kilometrów* from the one he grew up in, with its rusting scythes and uncovered well. At six years old he'd thought it a paradise, but his father had given him a beating after finding him playing there by himself. It was the only beating he had ever had, and now, looking at the boy, Jozef understood why his father had so feared for him all those years ago.

'I am allowed to know where it is?'

But TC shook his head. 'Nobody can. It's mine, and I'm never going to leave it. Never, ever.'

What was the point of telling the boy it would not be so? To Jozef the thought of the growing up TC would some day have to do—and of all the losses that would entail—was heartbreaking in its inevitability. If only there was some way to preserve the richness of these years to draw on in the bleaker, duller days ahead.

Yet perhaps that was just what Jozef himself had done; it was, after all, his memories of the farm that both sustained and tormented him, that kept sending him back, again and again, to the idea that a life without land was *not enough*. And anyway, who was he to wish TC forever a child, forever lost?

No, perhaps it was better to let it all go, Jozef conceded, as he watched the boy throw sticks for the dog. Perhaps it was better just to grow up and forget. Life would come for the boy in the end, and it would spit him out an adult, and what would any of this matter then?

14

PAG RAG DAY

It was the middle of May and TC had not spent a full day in school for over a week. He had been going more—he had been trying to. Jozef sometimes asked him, and he didn't like to lie; Jozef would look at him and he could tell he was disappointed. So he had been trying to go more, but now the weather was nice and there was too much going on, too much to miss. Sometimes he would leave at lunch; some mornings he would mean to go, but once he was out of the flat his mind would simply turn away from the idea of it, like a horse refusing a jump.

The school had sent a letter, but he found it easy enough to intercept it. He had worried about them phoning his mum, until he remembered she had lost her mobile a while back and now had a different number. And then he had let himself believe that nothing bad was going to happen.

But now there she was at the top of the stairwell, smoking, when he got in. She grabbed his arm and marched him through the front door and into the kitchen, a cigarette clamped in her fist.

'Why ain't you been going to school?'

'I have!'

'No you ain't. Don't you lie to me. I had them round here today.'

TC was silent, looked at the floor.

'Answer me!'

'I don't like it.'

'I don't care if you like it; until you're sixteen it ain't up to you. Now they say I'm going to get a fine. And you've been hiding their letters, don't tell me you ain't.' She stubbed the fag out in a saucer on the kitchen table. 'Where is it you're going all day, anyway?'

TC shrugged. 'Nowhere.'

She folded her arms and regarded him keenly. 'Skulking off by yourself, I bet. Why ain't you made any friends?'

'They're all weird.'

'Come off it. Why won't you play with the other kids?'

'They like different stuff, that's all.'

'Like what?'

'I don't know. *X Factor*. Football.'

'You used to like football.'

'Only cos Dad did. I liked playing with Dad.'

He wasn't crying, and then he was. She looked away, took a breath. Let it out.

'Listen. Your dad ain't coming back, OK? It's better this way; one day you'll understand. I'm doing my best. I got work now; there's food on the table. So it would be good if you made some friends, OK? Tried to fit in a bit. Then you'll enjoy it a bit more.'

'I don't like being shut up in the classrooms, Mum. I want to be outside.'

'When you're sixteen you can do what you like. Until then you just gotta try a bit harder, OK? I told them about your dad and they're going to help you catch up on what you've missed; special circumstances, they said. But I can't afford to pay any fine, TC, and I ain't having social services round here either. OK?'

TC nodded.

'Good. Right, I'm going to the shops. There's never any food in this fucking place.'

TC watched while she put her jacket on, fumbled for her keys. It was nothing like as bad as it might've been; yeah, she had been angry, but he had known it was coming, and in a way it was a relief. She seemed pleased it was over, too; a problem solved, he supposed.

Yet he wanted her to mention his dad again, ask him more things about school. He wanted to try and answer properly this time. 'Do you want me to come with you to the shop?' he asked.

She was at the door; looked round, surprised. 'If you want.'

TC followed her down the stairwell and out onto the litter-blown high road. He thought about what he could say, what she might like, what wouldn't get him in trouble. In the end, though, he didn't say anything, just walked along beside her, as though they were just mother and son, as though some kind of understanding had been reached.

As they neared the bookies', TC looked up and saw the old lady with the stick heading slowly towards them, and when they passed he gave her a grin that lit up his face. So he has someone, Sophia thought. That's something, at least.

The wind picked up, blowing dust and cigarette ends before them down the street, while overhead the swifts circled endlessly, tiny black scimitars feeding thirty storeys up above the city.

*   *   *

The party ended with the usual squeals and shrieks, but Linda's ears had learned to tune much of it out. The restaurant, one of a chain which had 'quirkiness' built into its marketing profile, was where all the kids were having their birthdays that year.

On the way back to the car she barely registered the overexcited chatter of Daisy and Susannah, who was coming back to play for a little while. She fiddled unsuccessfully with the air conditioning before giving up and opening her window. The chatter of starlings squabbling over bits of gherkin and lettuce from a dropped burger carton carried over the sound of the engine, over even the sound

146

of Daisy telling Susannah what they were going to do when they got home. It wasn't that her daughter was bossy, Linda told herself, more that the force of her imagination tended to carry others before her. Yes, it would have been good for her to have had siblings, but it was too late for that now. And it wasn't as though Susannah ever seemed to mind Daisy being in charge.

At home, she called hello to Steven who was working in the study, threw the car keys onto the kitchen worktop and followed the girls out into the garden. The day had started bright but had clouded over since lunchtime, though it was still humid and close.

Once so neat and symmetrical, the garden was definitely looking untidier since she had let the gardener go. For one thing there were a lot more weeds; she planned to ask Sophia about them next time she visited, but until then she wasn't sure which might be a plant, and so left them alone until they did something that made them easy to identify.

It was hard to let go of the image she had of how the garden should look—had looked, in fact: neat and stylish, everything just so. But it doesn't matter, she kept telling herself. It's the doing it that's important. It was what her father would have said.

Today she wanted to do some pruning. Several of the shrubs had become so bushy they had practically blended into each other and were crowding out the nicotiana and pinks she had planted—too few and too far apart—at their feet.

She fetched the canvas trug from the shed, a grey mouse shooting into the corner as she drew back the bolt. The nest now held seven tiny pink pups, the third litter to be raised in the shed so far that

147

year, and not the last. It was just as well, as the local cats and foxes, and the pair of sparrowhawks that sometimes visited the garden, saw to it that few survived long after venturing into the garden.

The air inside was dry and musty, with a particular stillness that wasn't dispelled by the sound of the two girls whispering behind it. The game they were playing seemed to involve hiding from Linda, and as she shut the shed door behind her and shot the bolt she remembered playing similar games in the park outside the estate with her brother. The aim would be to get from the benches to the chain-link fence without being seen by whoever was in the kitchen. Michael would pretend to be a commando, wriggling doggedly on his stomach, but Linda would watch her mother carefully as she moved about inside the flat and would dart from hiding place to hiding place when her head was turned. She never knew if she had won, as the moment that she touched the house Michael would decide that they had to go and storm a drawbridge, or spy on Blofeld, or land on the moon.

Linda took the secateurs and began attacking the choisya. There was probably a specific method she should follow, but it looked vigorous enough; it would surely survive. She had read that the cut stems smelled of basil, but to her they were more like cat. She threw them onto the grass behind her.

Next to the choisya was the area she had dug over for Daisy to have as her own. They had gone on a day trip to see the bluebells at a big National Trust property out of town, and on the way back Daisy had asked for her own flower bed. So Linda had marked out a bed a couple of metres long,

148

ruthlessly rooting up French lavender, stachys and several allium corms, and the next day had edged it with little rolls of split logs. She had pictured neat rows of seedlings, the two of them tending the bed together, and to that end had bought Daisy several packets of seeds: forget-me-nots, sweet williams and nasturtiums, chives, salad leaves and rocket. But so far none of them had gone into the ground, and weeds were coming up instead.

'She'll do it in her own time,' Steven reassured her. 'Don't make it a chore.' He was right, Linda knew; and anyway, there was no sense in feeling snubbed. At nine years old now and with a houseful of toys, only Daisy's desire for a kitten had lasted longer than a couple of months. That, and her correspondence with her grandmother.

Sophia's letters often came by post, Daisy taking her replies with her when she visited her grandmother. Sometimes she would ask her mother for help with a long word, but for the most part Linda had little idea what they wrote to each other about.

'Mummy, when will it rain?' asked Daisy now. Linda stood back and looked critically at the choisya. Her daughter was gazing fiercely at the sky, one grubby hand shading her eyes, Susannah like a grave little shadow behind her.

'I don't know, darling. Why?'

'We need the worms to come up and they only come up when it rains,' sighed Daisy. 'I'm going to ask Daddy,' and she ran inside, leaving Susannah hesitating on the lawn.

'Why do you need worms, Susie?' Linda asked. 'Is it for a game?'

'No, it's . . .'

149

'Not a game.' Linda's mind was half on the choisya, now showing rather more of its pale trunk than she had planned.

'For mud pies. Daisy says worm casts are the best kind of mud. Her granny told her.' And with that Susannah ran off after Daisy into the house.

The sudden rush of memory sent Linda's hand to her chest. Of course! You collected the worm casts in the morning and mixed them with a little water, and you got the smoothest mud, without any bits in it. Then you put it in fairy-cake cases and let them dry in the sun. The little grey cakes were suddenly so vivid to her, stacked on the flat's outside windowsills to dry; and there was a feeling to the memory, too, of her and her mummy doing something together, and it being nice. Why had she never thought to show Daisy how to make them herself?

She had a vision of the little park in blazing summer, Michael pedalling away from her across the cracked, straw-brown grass in the tin jeep Dad had painted with old gloss paint because it rusted, herself a little girl making a house for her Womble behind the benches. And there was the little bike she and Michael shared, with its fat white tyres, and her mother's gardening gloves, shaped by long use like carapaces of her strong brown hands.

And there, of course, was her father: sanding the spindles of a chair-back at the side of the flats, or sitting inside in his favourite chair with his evening drink. How proud she had been when he taught her to make a Tom Collins: two ice cubes, a finger of gin, a little Jif lemon, some icing sugar and then soda water to the top. Mother preferred a whisky soda, and would make it herself.

Nothing was ever lost, she reflected, and wondered what Daisy would remember from her own early years. Making a snowman together, perhaps? Though you didn't get to choose.

Before going inside she carried the pile of cuttings to the heap at the back of the garden. On the back wall of the house the barometer was falling.

*   *   *

The rain began quite suddenly, while she was making supper. Steven came in from dropping Susie home and switched the kitchen light on, and Linda realised it had grown dim outside. Then came the rain, fat drops that darkened the patio and ran down the window in sheets. A distant flicker of lightning brought Daisy scuttling downstairs from her room.

'I like storms,' she announced staunchly, to no one in particular. Linda rattled the saucepan lid over the sound of the thunder.

But no more came. While they were eating the rain thinned to a patter and then petered out, and as the breeze picked up it tore a ragged hole in the cloud, a low sun returning to light up the sparkling garden in which every living corner dripped and steamed.

Steven opened the back door and breathed in petrichor, the rich green smell that follows rain. On the gable above him a blackbird shook the rain from its feathers and cocked a beady eye down at the sunlit lawn where worms rose and weeds were sending down secret roots, and where tomorrow a small girl would set about the worm

151

casts before breakfast with a bucket and spade.

*   *   *

After Daisy had been persuaded to bed, Steven and Linda sat at the kitchen table with a bottle of Bordeaux and the back door open, watching as the last of the light drained from the sky. Linda wore an old cardigan of her mother's, left there after a visit, and picked at the earth under her fingernails. 'My hands look the oldest,' she said, holding one out for Steven's inspection. 'They're even worse than my neck.'

'Don't be silly. They're perfectly fine.'

'All right for you to say, you're the Younger Man,' she replied, the soubriquet so old now it was threadbare. Still, though, he smiled.

'Ten years is nothing. I'm a man, I'll still die first.'

Like Dad, Linda thought, but didn't say it. 'Do you think she should have had brothers and sisters?'

'Maybe, maybe not. Why are you worrying about it again?'

'I'm not worrying. I was just thinking about Michael today. We used to play together, you know? All the time.'

'She's got plenty of friends to play with.'

'I know, but it's different with siblings. You have to get along. And you have to share. You don't get everything your own way.'

'You think she's spoiled.'

'No, I just think ... it's just her and us, you know? She gets all our time, all our attention.'

'Paradise, I'd say.'

152

'Well, now it is, I'm sure. But maybe there should be more people in her life.'

'There's your mother.'

'That's not what I meant; I meant people to share us with. Mum's a grown-up.'

'Hardly.'

'What do you mean, hardly? She's still got all her faculties, you know.'

'I know, I didn't mean that. I meant she's more like a friend to Daisy. They're as bad as each other half the time.'

Linda was silent.

'I don't mean she does any harm, love,' said Steven. 'It's lovely that Daisy gets on with her gran.'

'I know,' Linda sighed. 'I know. It's just . . . I look at them, and I wish that things were better. Easier. You know, with me and Mum. I love her—of course I do—but when we're together it's like—it's like—'

'I know, love,' said Steven. 'But she doesn't mean to rub you up the wrong way. She's just . . . forthright. She means well, you know that. She loves you, darling—' but Linda looked away.

*   *   *

The wine was low in the bottle, and it was fully dark outside. Steven fetched some notepaper from the study and handed it to Linda. 'Your mum's handwriting is getting worse, so Daisy asked me to help read it. Go on.'

It was Sophia's most recent letter. *'Dear Daisy,'* it began,

I have found where the swifts are nesting. They are in the tower of St Francis's Church! It's not a very high tower, but it's got lots of nooks and crannies for them to get in and out. Have your baby swallows fledged yet?

You mustn't worry about the hedgehog. It's summer and he will be roaming far and wide, eating slugs and snails and having adventures. You probably won't see him again until the days get shorter and he starts to think about finding somewhere to hibernate. Your garden is definitely his favourite, but I think he probably visits a few different ones near you as well.

There are a lot of grey squirrels about at the moment. They are very playful, especially the younger ones. They can do acrobatic tricks like tumbling and hanging by their back feet. Yesterday I saw one steal someone's lunch! A man was sitting on the benches eating a sandwich. He put half of it on the bench next to him, and the next moment it was gone. He looked very cross, but the squirrel must have been very pleased with itself. It took it up a tree to eat, and two crows made off with the pieces of lettuce that had fallen out.

And of course there are my chiffchaffs. The chicks are still doing well and it won't be long before they fledge. They all crane out of the nest with their gapes (mouths) open, begging to be fed. They look like little dinosaurs.

Now, our flower bed project. What is coming up in yours? In my patch I can see lots of fat hen seedlings, some yellow corydalis, a dandelion, two foxgloves (I planted their parents, years ago!) and one little speedwell. There is also something

154

else, a mysterious seedling that I haven't identified yet. We will have to wait and see what it turns into.

The corydalis is interesting because it isn't really a weed, but it seems to grow everywhere around here so it gets treated like one by most people. It just goes to show that a weed really is any plant growing in the wrong place. Dandelion seeds are airborne, as you know, and fat hen seeds are too, so we know how they got here. The speedwell seed was probably dormant (sleeping) in the soil. The corydalis seeds might have been carried in by ants. The seed has a tasty part which the ants like, but once they've eaten it the rest of the seed is free to grow. Isn't that clever?

It will be interesting to see whether you get different seedlings growing in your flower bed from those I get in mine. Perhaps you could do me a drawing of what you can see, and next time I visit you we can look at it together.

With all my love, sweet pea,
Granny xx

Linda got up to close the back door, taking a few extra moments with the bolts.

'Lovely, isn't it?' prompted Steven.

'Yes, of course.'

'What is it?'

'Nothing. It's just . . . *sweet pea*.'

'Did she use to call you that?'

Linda returned to the table, leaned on the back of her chair. 'No, Dad did. When I was very small.'

Steven smiled. 'Well, that's a lovely thing, then, isn't it? Don't you think?'

'Yes . . . I know.' She picked up the bottle and

155

glasses, exhaled.

'You still miss your dad, don't you?' Steven said.

Linda gazed out at the dark garden. 'I've been thinking about him a lot recently; I'm not sure why. You know he used to take me on nature walks?'

Steven nodded. 'Like your mum does with Daisy.'

'Yes. And now we know what she's up to with that ruddy flower bed!'

'I know! Little horror.' Steven grinned, relieved to see Linda's wry smile. 'She could have told you why she didn't want to plant any of the seeds you bought her.'

'It's a good project, though, isn't it? Just like Mum.'

'It's an excellent project. Do you think we're allowed to know about it?'

'Well, you are.'

'I don't think she meant to keep it secret from you. I think she just forgot.'

'Maybe.'

'Why don't we ask her about it tomorrow?'

*   *   *

All night the wind gusted and fell, gusted and fell, clouds passing invisibly overhead in a black sky. Just before dawn rain fell again, but by the time the blackbird took up his position on the roof the sky was pale and clear. He opened his yellow beak and sang Sunday in on a cartwheel of notes.

15

OAK DAY

Jozef's back was hot under the hi-vis vest, but the earth was damp and cool beneath his knees. He knelt carefully between the busy lizzies and pulled up bindweed and creeping buttercup from the back of the semicircular bed.

One morning, out with Znajda on the common, he had seen the Park Ranger van parked up near the railway tunnel, and had sat on a nearby wall smoking roll-ups until the two men in their green trousers and sweatshirts returned.

'Sorry, mate,' they'd said, shaking their heads, and he had felt foolish for thinking things could be that easy. But then one of them had rolled down the van's window as they pulled away and suggested he try a contractor, and so he found a couple of numbers. On his second call he was asked to go for an interview; he had been nervous, a little, but it turned out they just wanted willing hands and weren't too bothered about his English; his agricultural experience, which he had rehearsed over and over in his head on the way there, was not even required.

A few days later he had his first shift. The worst part was litter picking and emptying the dog bins, but there was a landscaping team, and courses you could go on in arboriculture and biodiversity, and at the back of his mind there was a cautious hope, one he didn't dare look at too closely, that perhaps he could find a way forward. Each night when he showered he watched the good earth leave his body in the water. Yet more remained, he felt, driven deep and invisibly under his skin.

This particular park was unfamiliar to him, and more formal than the common's casual acres, but it was still good to be outside again, among living things. They broke for lunch, afterwards riding in the van to a scrubby triangle of land between a storage depot and a supermarket. It was hardly a park, yet there was a sign at the entrance with a little map and a surprisingly long list of the living things that depended on it.

Their task was to clear a pond. It was choked with flags, the water between them blood-warm and bright green; above it flew banded demoiselles, as darkly iridescent as petrol. Feeling his way into the water in thigh-high waders, Jozef hit something hard and straight with his shin. Hauling it out, streaming water and weed, he saw it was an iron crucifix three feet tall.

He laid it on the grass as around him the talk turned to a .303 rifle once recovered from a canal. Jozef looked at the innocent surface of the water and tried to imagine what circumstance had led to a cross being dumped—or hidden, or lost—in the pond in this peaceable country. Whose hands had been last to hold it, and when? These things were lost to time. He worked on, pulling from the water armful after armful of blanket weed and the occasional slick wriggle of a newt, while on the bank the crucifix dried rust-coloured and brittle in the sun and swifts screamed urgently to each other, high and faint, far overhead.

*   *   *

Sophia was setting the tea things out. She unfolded a tea towel, looked at it critically: it was freshly ironed, spotless, but threadbare in places. She found another. The teapot was ready by the kettle, and she filled up the striped jug with milk and reached the biscuits down from the cupboard, putting six, this time, on a plate, and setting two mugs next to it. Linda was coming over, with Daisy—'for tea', she had said. Silly to be nervous. Her own daughter, for goodness' sakes.

She sat at the kitchen table and looked out at the little park. How different from Daisy Linda had been at that age. Daisy was indulged, yes, and more protected, but also so much more confident about her place in the world. Linda had always worried too much about what other people thought, even as a little girl. Was that right, or was that hindsight?

And she herself was different, too. She was much more affectionate with Daisy than she had been with Linda; somehow it was easier. It made her wish that she could have her time with Linda again; but also glad, in a way, that all the worrying was over and that she could love the little girl easily, without any of the cost that being a mother entailed. And she had been a good mother, hadn't she? Linda seemed happy with her life; she had certainly bettered herself. Goodness only knows how much money she made. Pots, probably. Steven too. What did any of it matter now? Sophia wasn't sure. Her children may have made different choices from her, but they were both doing well; both, it seemed, were happy. What more, then, did she want for them?

She looked out of the window to where the

little Turkish man from the takeaway was smoking a cigarette on the benches. He was a nice chap; they had once had a very good conversation about folk stories, and he had sung her a beautiful and mournful *türkü*.

There they were, her daughter and granddaughter, walking together into the park from Leasow Road. Her heart gave a jump, and for a moment she put her hand to her chest, but the palpitations didn't come and she let out a long, slow breath. Daisy was running ahead and waving, and Sophia got up to let them in.

Daisy clasped her legs and put her face up for a kiss. Behind her, Linda looked . . . tense, somehow. She kissed Sophia and hugged her for a moment longer than usual. The thought came to Sophia that perhaps Linda was ill—or Daisy was. Surely not. They wouldn't tell her like this.

'Come in, come in—I've just put the kettle on,' she said. In fact, she had boiled it twice, waiting, and now worried that the water might taste odd. 'Let's sit in here, shall we?'

Daisy had already run into the sitting room and installed herself in Henry's chair. '*Ohhww*,' she groaned, 'we *never* sit in the nice room.'

'Daisy!' said Linda. 'All the rooms are nice.' She looked embarrassed.

'Goodness me, Linda,' said Sophia, 'I shouldn't worry. I don't.'

Linda smiled and took off her coat. 'No, you're right. Sorry.'

'Come on, sweet pea,' Sophia called to Daisy, 'come and sit with us. I've got biscuits!'

Linda sat down at the kitchen table with its checked cloth, and Sophia brought the tray over.

160

'Goodness,' she said, picking up one of the mugs with its faded design, 'I remember these. I can't believe you've still got them! Well, I know what we'll be getting you for Christmas.'

Sophia smiled and looked away.

'So, how are you, Mum?' Linda asked. There wasn't really any other way to begin.

'I'm well, thank you,' Sophia replied, wondering if they were going to have A Talk. 'Shall I be mother?'

Daisy was swinging her legs under the table and grinning up at both of them. 'Can I have a juice box?' she said.

'Can I have a juice box . . . ?' said Linda.

'. . . *please*.'

'Yes, darling—there's one in your backpack,' she replied. 'Go and fetch it. And there are pens and pencils, too.'

Daisy took two biscuits and scrambled down from the table. 'I'm going in the nice room,' she called out. 'I won't spill anything, I promise.'

Linda wrapped her hands around her mug and stared down at it. 'The park's looking nice,' she said. Sophia raised her eyebrows. 'I mean it!' Linda continued. 'Those trees are out—what are they?'

'Ah, *Prunus padus*. Pretty, aren't they?'

'The white ones. They're lovely. And the herb robert's flowering.'

'Goodness me, you have been doing your homework.' The remark came out tarter than Sophia had meant, and she smiled, to soften it.

'I have, I've been looking things up.'

'Have you indeed? What's brought this on?'

'And I got rid of the gardener; I'm doing it myself now. I thought maybe you could give me

161

some advice about things, when you're next over. Or just come over. If you wanted.'

'I'd be happy to, love. Just name the day—I'm sure I'll be free.'

Linda paused, looked out of the window. 'Mum, are you . . . are you happy?'

'Happy? Of course,' replied Sophia, looking at her daughter with concern. 'I'm fine. I miss your dad, of course, and your brother doesn't phone often enough, but you know that.'

'Yes, of course . . .' but she didn't sound too sure. 'Of course. Are you . . . lonely?'

'Lonely? No, I don't think so. I don't have time to be lonely. I think lonely means bored, doesn't it? Or nearly. You're all round the corner, which is lovely, and in between times I'm certainly never bored.'

Linda looked at her as though she found that hard to believe; Sophia reminded herself that, to those who need their days to be full of tasks and commitments, the lives of those without such things often seems barren, when in fact it can be rich and full. There seemed so much they didn't understand about each other, but no easy way to bridge the gap. Yet she could see that her daughter was trying.

'I'm fine, love, you mustn't worry,' she said, putting her hand over Linda's on the table. 'But it's nice that you asked. And how about you—how is work? And Steven?'

'Yes, all fine,' Linda replied. That clearly wasn't what had brought her here. 'But I've been thinking about . . . about when we were little, and Dad, and you of course. That's all.'

That meant everything, a lifetime of love and misunderstandings. Sophia wondered where her daughter would begin, and whether she really wanted her to.

'I remembered Dad saying something,' Linda said haltingly. 'Well, lots of things, obviously. But this one thing: "We are the clay that grew tall." Do you remember that, do you remember him saying that, at all?'

'Did he now?' said Sophia. 'It doesn't ring a bell. I think it must be a poem, or the Bible. Have you tried looking it up?'

'Of course. I've been on the Internet and everything, but I can't find it,' replied Linda. 'What do you think it means?'

'I expect he meant that we are made of the same stuff as the earth, knowing Henry,' said Sophia, her expression soft. 'You know—we're not any different, not separate from it. It's in our blood and our bones. You'd say he was a hippie or something, nowadays, but it wasn't that. He just felt people were better off noticing the world around them, and the seasons, than *not* noticing—that it made their lives richer. We tried to set an example to you two, but you can't force it; that's the thing with children.'

'But sometimes it's just about having the time,' said Linda. 'There's a lot more going on these days than when Dad was a boy, you know? The world's full of stuff all shouting for your attention. You can't watch over every last sparrow.'

'I know, love. But the things you really bother with in life loom large, you see, so you do well to choose them wisely. Oh, I know everything's supposed to be equally good these days and nobody's in the wrong. But that's rot. Some things help you grow, and some are just—just empty, like too many sweets. You have to choose what to notice, or your life will get filled up with the wrong things—Daisy's, too.'

'You're saying I should be bringing her up differently? You're saying I should be like you were, with us?'

Linda's eyes were on her mug, but there was an edge in her voice that Sophia knew well. She wondered, as she often did, why her daughter resented her; what it was that she had got so wrong. Perhaps they should have it out; perhaps, but not today, not when things had been going so well. 'No, love,' she said, reaching out for her daughter's arm, 'I'm not saying that at all; at least, I don't mean to. I suppose I'm just trying to explain to you what your dad and I wanted for you; what we were trying to do.'

*   *   *

Daisy was bored with drawing, and in two minds about having her mum there. Usually she had her granny to herself and they played pretend, or she told her granny about things and her granny asked her questions. Not about school, or homework, but what she liked doing and what she thought about things. She wasn't ignored, usually.

She took her drawing into the kitchen and stood at Sophia's elbow. Sophia put her arm around her, absent-mindedly, but they kept on talking. 'I've drawn a bee house,' she announced, and Sophia took the drawing from her, but she didn't look at it, not properly.

'Look,' Daisy said, and began to stab at it with the orange pencil.

164

'In a moment, sweet pea,' said her granny, which was new.

'Daisy, darling, why don't you go and draw me another one?' said Linda, which was silly because it wasn't even for her. 'Mummy and Gran are talking.'

'Make it a picture of something really horrible,' said Sophia, giving her a wink. 'The worst thing you can think of.' And she patted Daisy's bottom, and that, Daisy knew, meant go away.

The orange pencil had got blunt and there wasn't a sharpener, so she couldn't even draw an explosion. Daisy sat cross-legged in her grandmother's chair and scowled. It wasn't fair. They were still talking, now about the olden days: something about games and her uncle Mike, who she couldn't properly remember. 'I wish I was at home,' she said, out loud.

She got up and went to the window and breathed on it so she could write a rude word backwards. But then she saw him: TC. He had his head down and was hugging the back boundary of the park, behind the oaks; he seemed to be trying to slip through unobserved. 'I can see you,' she whispered. Where was he going so secretly?

She did hesitate, for a moment, in the kitchen doorway, but neither woman looked over. And she was only going to be a minute or two; she was only going to say hello.

It was the sound of the latch that gave her away. 'Daisy?' called her mother. Sophia had her hand to her chest; for a moment, just for a moment, she had thought it was Henry, letting himself in.

'Daisy!' Linda was up and in the hall, her face like thunder. 'Get back in here this instant! What on earth do you think you're doing?'

165

Daisy's face was flushed. 'I was just . . . I was just . . .'

Linda held her by the arm and shook her. 'By yourself!' she shouted. 'Where?'

'To the park, I was going to come straight back,' Daisy said, and began to cry.

Sophia got up and laid a hand on Linda's arm. 'Perhaps—'

'No perhaps! She was going to go off, by herself, without telling us. She's nine! *Nine!*'

This was not the moment to remind Linda that she herself had played in the park at nine years old. Sophia could see she would have to talk to her daughter about it, might even have to admit that she had allowed Daisy to play in the park without her once—more than once—and so at least some of the blame, if there was to be any, was hers. Not now, though. Today had been precious, and she didn't want to spoil it.

Linda turned back to Daisy. 'What were you thinking, Daisy? Well?'

The little girl turned to her grandmother for help, but Sophia could only look away.

16

HAYMAKING

The grass around the edges of the common had been left unmowed and had grown tall and thronged with seed heads. While the mown part was just grass, where it was left long it was possible to tell what that grass was actually made up of, as lesser timothy, rye, meadow fescue, cocksfoot, sweet vernal and foxtail all put up their differing banners, and sweet white clover brought the bees beneath. Over by the oaks the elegant, sandy feathers of tall oat grass floated above the finer, reddish inflorescence of the common bent below, like the two lengths of pelt on a cat.

Once, right across the country, the meadows would have been scythed at around this time of year, the hay left to dry in long, fragrant windrows. Turned by hand, it would have been pitched up with forks onto a wagon and towed to the rick by horsepower.

The heavy horses have gone, most of the hedgerows grubbed up and the fields they encircled lost in the huge swathes demanded by agribusiness—as though the enclosures had never happened, but with no return of the land to common use. Now, mechanical balers leave neat packages of wrapped silage in their wake.

The old names for each of the fields are more or less forgotten, but so is the hardship which enslaved generations. Here and there in the countryside the old barns survive, made sleek with fixtures and fittings and with sports cars parked outside. In forgotten corners of the more dilapidated sort of going concern, ancient flails and tillers rust and rot down, returning themselves with each season to the earth.

*   *   *

A day like today could not be spent indoors, and despite his promise to his mum, despite Jozef, TC did not even consider going to school. Everything

167

was alive, everything was happening: flowers, new butterflies, fledging birds. He didn't want to miss a moment of it.

He went to the common first. It was bisected by both a railway line and a road, and while he could find his way around its four sections and the surrounding streets without hesitation, if he had been asked to draw the different parts— the oak wood, the sports field, the thickets by the cutting, the avenue of planes—and show how they related to each other, he could not have done it. His knowledge was detailed beyond measure, but inchoate.

Now he took the path that ran alongside the embankment, where few people went because it wasn't really a short cut to anywhere. Beside the path the thistles stood four feet high, and the wall barley was turning golden. The brambles were coming into flower, he saw, white and grubby pink, promising a good blackberry season to come.

He came off the path and walked through the tall grass, dipping his hands into it as though into water and every so often pulling the pale seeds from a stem to make a tight, dry bunch between his fingers. I'm planting it, he thought, as he let the seeds fly. Next year more will grow because of me.

Out on the pitches Jozef leaned on his elbows and gazed at TC through half-closed eyes. His shift didn't start until after lunch, and he was taking Znajda for a walk. He watched as TC moved through the long grass, the sun lighting the side of his face and turning his skin golden. Not in school again. He felt hurt, somehow. He wondered where the boy was going, and what it was that he reminded him of, walking away from him like that through the long grass.

Before work the previous day he had waited on the benches in the little park until the old lady, Sophia, emerged from the estate, as she did most mornings at about the same time. He'd wanted to talk to her about the boy, about what people might think of their friendship; maybe ask her what she thought about teaching him to whittle.

'You see a lot of him, now?' she had asked, and Jozef had nodded. 'Well, sometimes. A couple of times a week. I—I worry about him, if he has food, you know.'

'Well, thank goodness there's somebody looking out for him, then. There's a mother, I think, though it could be a sister. Or perhaps he's in foster care, poor boy.'

'You think it's OK—it's normal—that we see each other?'

'My granddaughter is nine, I'll have you know, and she's my best friend. Age shouldn't matter, not if you get on.'

It wasn't quite what he had meant, but he didn't know how to be more explicit. And then she had asked him about his uniform, and he had told her about his new job in the parks, and when he got up to go he had quite forgotten to bring up the subject of whittling at all.

Now he folded his jacket behind his head and dozed until Znajda's shadow fell across him. She was sniffing idly at the grass, privy to a whole world of information he could only guess at. He raised himself on his elbows and said her name, but she merely looked at him for a moment before trotting purposefully off towards the path that ran through the oak woods. She clearly wanted to carry on with her walk, and Jozef got up and ambled after her.

He caught up with her at the fallen tree, its graffiti now faded to near-invisibility. She picked her way through the clitter of sawn-up logs before tucking herself adroitly into a little cave beneath the massive trunk and squinting up into the sundazzle as though she had lain there a hundred times before—and perhaps she had. She put her tongue out and panted at Jozef who stood, one foot on a section of branch, and looked down speculatively at her.

*   *   *

TC stayed on the common all day. He lay in the long grass and put one eye at ground level, looking for the little channels left by mice and voles. He followed bees from flower to flower, and when he got hungry he thought of Znajda, and looked in the bins. Lots of people were eating their lunch outdoors in the nice weather, and he found a half-finished Oasis and a panini oozing with melted cheese that had hardly even been touched.

The afternoon smelled of pollen, was accompanied by birdsong and seemed to go on forever and ever. At last a mackerel sky turned pink as dusk fell, and bats began to flicker above the footpaths. They roosted in the cool, damp shadows under the railway bridge and along the embankment, and feasted on moths at night. Hearing them was like looking at a very faint star; not so much seeing—not so much hearing—as something else, as though the knowledge came through a medium other than mere senses.

TC climbed his favourite tree to wait for all the

night-time creatures to appear. Below him came the after-work joggers and evening dog walkers, and then two older estate kids with their dog, speaking a muttered patois he only half understood. It was a fighting dog—a bit like Znajda, maybe, but the colour of sharp sand, bigger and with longer legs. One kid held it back with a chain and a leather harness, letting the dog strain against it as they walked. The dog was amped up, wired, and TC drew his legs up onto the branch, quietly.

But instead of passing on they veered off the main path and took a little trail through the brambles which led to a clearing beneath the oaks; there one of them rolled a spliff while the one with the dog made a phone call. His jeans were so low; TC wondered how they didn't fall down, and whether one day he would wear his jeans like that. The kids—they weren't kids, he could see now, not schoolkids anyway—they had caps on under their hoods, both caps the same. Did that mean something? He wasn't sure.

They had a knotted bit of rope and they gave it to the dog to play tug of war with. The dog gripped the rope with its teeth and shook its head from side to side; you could hear it growling and you could see the kid's arms that were holding the rope getting jerked from side to side. TC didn't like it; he wanted to get down, but there was no way of doing it, not without them seeing him. He wondered about going further up into the oak, but it was getting darker all the time, and he didn't know the handholds; and if he fell down the dog would get him.

The dog wouldn't let go of the rope and so one of the kids took a stick from the back of his jeans. It looked like the handle of a hammer, but it was flattened at one end. He hit the dog on its shoulders, but it still wouldn't let go. Then the other one put the dog between his knees and they forced the stick in its mouth and got the rope out. They lifted the stick up and the dog's forelegs went up too. It kept growling, a low growl, but it wasn't trying to get away; maybe it thought it was a game, maybe it was all just playing. It didn't feel like playing, though.

They kicked the dog and after a bit it let go of the stick and stood there, panting. Then TC saw that they were looking up; he froze, his heart thumping. Had they heard him, somehow? Had he made a noise?

But it wasn't his tree they were looking at. They dragged the yellow dog by its chain over to the oak next to his and one of them pulled a branch down; they made the dog bite the branch. Then they let it go. The branch swung up and the dog hung there, kicking, yelping, growling. TC felt sick or like crying. It was horrible to watch, it was like they were hanging it. Why? The dog went limp for a moment, but it wouldn't let go. Then it struggled and growled again. He thought about Znajda, tried to picture someone doing that to her, but it was too awful so he stopped. She wouldn't let them, anyway. Jozef wouldn't either, no way.

TC couldn't stop looking, he couldn't stop. He didn't see the other kids come until they were right in the clearing. They had a dog too, a bit smaller and darker; it began baying and lunging at the yellow dog, and had to be dragged back, half choking, by its chain. They were all smoking weed, and the sweet, familiar smell drifted up to TC

172

where he sat. The embers glowed red when each spliff was inhaled, then the spark arced downwards with each arm. The yellow dog kicked and growled where it hung from the branch; they kept the darker one a bit away and held his head and looked at its teeth. They were all talking, excited. TC felt sick.

They turned back to the yellow dog. The kid with the stick got it out again and landed it a blow on the back of the neck; it let go of the branch with a yelp—but when it hit the ground the other dog went for it, dragging the chain out of its owner's hand, the two animals locked together in a sudden and terrifying frenzy. Then it was all yelping and shouting, all of them trying to pull the dogs apart, trying to grab the chain, the kid with the stick wielding it over and over, the dull, sickening thumps as it fell and all the fine young grass of the clearing torn up in a wide circle as the dogs' dark blood flicked out to spatter the surrounding trees.

*   *   *

When TC came down from the tree it was proper night. Before leaving he snapped off the twig he had tied in a knot all those months ago. It had been a stupid idea; there was no point in it.

He didn't think about anything as he left the wood. He didn't look at the torn-up earth, or the wounded trees. He tried not to think about the dogs. Their faces, when they were finally separated, had been ruined: swollen, bloody, torn. They didn't look scary any more, they looked pitiful. One had to be carried; both of them looked sad, and somehow ashamed. It all felt familiar to TC, as though it had all happened before.

173

He made for the secret garden. Such things could not exist in there.

He crawled under the rhododendron, where the fox sometimes slept. He imagined it would not begrudge him a night there. Ivy had crawled up and over much of it, making a kind of bower. He breathed the fox smell in, curled into it, and closed his eyes.

Around the sleeping boy the garden slowly resettled itself, but beyond that the vast city winked and glittered, the grass pollen, unchanged for millennia, settling invisibly over everything like a cloud.

17

MIDSUMMER

Warm and humid air moved in from France, then dry air slid above it from the plateaus of Spain. The June skies turned low and grey; the upper atmosphere cooled, and the weather became unpredictable.

Jozef was scouring the high road for Flat 131A, fat raindrops splashing on the warm pavement and down his neck. It didn't make sense; there were big gaps in the numbers, and it didn't help that most of the shops didn't display a number at all. He checked the plastic key ring again and decided to retrace his steps.

Finally he found a puddled alley that led off the high road and turned at right angles to run behind the shops for several hundred yards. Metal staircases led up from it to the flat roofs that formed the rear elevation of the shops, and a row of front doors—back doors, really—gave access to the flats above at first-floor level.

The alley housed the shops' huge metal bins. Most had flattened boxes stacked around them, and there was quite a lot of litter and old fruit. Jozef thought of rats, and hurried up the clanging stairs.

Number 131 had a faded pink door that had probably once been red; two long-dead tiger palms in plastic pots stood outside. He tried the key, and pushed the door open cautiously.

The little hall was dark, and the light didn't work. Jozef left the front door open so he could see which of the three inner doors was Flat A, pizza flyers slipping and whispering under his trainers.

The bedsit smelled a little stale, but it was better than he had expected. The main room had a divan base, but no mattress, a low table and a storage heater, and there was a little kitchen to one side and a bathroom with a shower curtain decorated with fish.

The main room looked out onto the high road; the kitchen and bathroom were windowless. Jozef tried to picture the shape of the original flat before it had been subdivided, but you'd have to have a look at the other two bedsits if you wanted to be sure.

He wondered what the neighbours were like; maybe Agata could tell him. It was she who had found him the place, really; she'd overheard one of the customers at the cafe complaining about a tenant and had introduced them. The landlord was a big man from Łódz´ with one eye, whom Jozef had instinctively liked. Znajda had too, struggling up into a lopsided sit from her place under Jozef's table to nose at the man's broad hand. Jozef left the cafe in the small hours with the man's phone number in his wallet, and a week later he had the key.

Outside there was a distant rumble, and a downpour beat a tattoo on the glass. Jozef looked out; he was above the halal butcher's, he worked out, the minimarket to the left. If he put his forehead to the glass and craned to the right he could see the old lady, Sophia, making her slow way through the little park towards her flat.

He closed his eyes for a moment. It wasn't the farm; it wasn't even his. But it was something.

*　　　*　　　*

An hour later Sophia was still sitting in the kitchen and looking out of her window at the rain. Saturday: she was due at Linda and Steven's for lunch, but at this rate she'd be wet through by the time she got there.

Eventually it eased, although the sky remained grey and low overhead. She put on a coat—not Henry's, her own—and the shoes Linda had bought her, and went back out.

In the little park blackbirds ran, paused and ran, and wrens shouted alarums from the undergrowth. The water on the high road fizzed under the buses' tyres. Sophia hunched her shoulders and tried to pick up her pace.

On Leasow Road she rang the doorbell and heard it chime sonorously deep inside the house. The front door was dove grey; at first she'd thought it an undercoat, and had been surprised to discover it was staying like that. Now she had got used to it, though, she had to admit it looked rather smart.

Linda answered the door just as the rain began to ease and embraced her gently, as though she were a bird—or perhaps it was just that she was wet. 'Hello, Mum,' she said. 'Here, let me take your coat.'

Sophia handed over a bread bag, tied at the top with string. 'For you.'

'What on earth is it?'

'Seeds,' she replied, taking off her coat with some difficulty. 'And a cutting. Honeysuckle. I did it just now, coming up your road. Do you have a pot and some compost? Only we don't want it to dry out.'

'You took it from someone's front garden? You stole it?'

'Yes, I suppose so.'

After a moment, Linda laughed. 'OK then, why not. I think the rain's stopped. Shall we?'

They went into the back garden. 'Here it is,' said Linda, dragging a plastic sack to the teak garden table. 'Is here all right? I don't have a potting bench.'

'Oh, fine. Got a pot?'

Linda fetched one from the shed, and Sophia showed her how to cut the woody stem diagonally, just below a bud, and push it gently into the half-filled pot. Some cling film and a rubber band finished the job.

'Lovely. Leave it in the shade and keep an eye on it. Don't let it dry out, or get mouldy. It should root within a fortnight.'

'Then what?'

'Well, then you've got yourself a new plant, free.'

'You mean—that's it?'

'I do. And your neighbour's is none the worse for it, so it's all . . . hunky-dory. Or whatever.'

Linda made tea and they took a tour of the garden, Linda pointing out plants whose names she didn't know, or that she had questions about. Sophia found it was lovely to be asked, lovely to be useful, and if she sometimes sounded more certain than she felt it was only because she was so enjoying her daughter's attention. She made a mental note to look up one or two things in her plant encyclopedia when she got home, just to be sure. Though it would be awful to have to admit she'd got it wrong.

Daisy was at Susannah's house, so lunch was just the three of them. Linda made salmon fishcakes with a rocket salad, and Steven emerged from the study to make a vinaigrette.

'People think of rocket as being exotic,' said Sophia, between mouthfuls, 'but it's been grown in this country for centuries. The medievals had it. Did you know that?'

Linda shook her head.

'Not that there's anything wrong with a nice gem lettuce, in my opinion. Do you remember your father's little gems? He grew a good lettuce, your father.'

'I remember his radishes,' said Linda. 'Oh, how I used to hate them.'

'No you didn't, you loved them! You're thinking of . . . of . . .'

'I'm not, Mum, I'm thinking of radishes. They always looked so wonderful—the pretty leaves with their red veins, and then the little radish like a ruby in the dust. But it was like eating a raw onion. I used to pick them out.'

'Rot. I wouldn't have let you.'

'You didn't, as I remember. Me and Michael used to sneak them into our pockets.'

'Did Linda tell you we're thinking of growing some vegetables?' Steven interrupted smoothly. 'I know it's a bit late for this year, but we thought there might be time for some chard and some carrots, perhaps some garlic, later.'

'Where?'

'Here, in the garden.'

'Well, I don't know about that. Why don't you get an allotment? Much better.'

'There are waiting lists these days,' Steven replied. 'It's become rather fashionable.'

'What, vegetables?'

'Growing your own, yes.'

Sophia was silent a moment. 'Well, that's good, I think,' she said. 'Gracious, your father's come back into fashion! How he'd laugh.'

She got up from the table and began opening the kitchen cupboards, coming back to the table with a bottle of ketchup. 'Sorry, Steven. The fishcakes were crying out for it,' she said.

'Not at all.'

Linda briefly closed her eyes.

'So where do you think we should put our vegetable patch?' Steven asked.

'Well, which side gets the most sun?'

'The left—but that's where Daisy's flower bed is. You know, the one—'

'The one she's doing with me, the one where we were going to see what germinated naturally. Only she isn't; I'm not sure she's really—what is it? *on board* with the idea. I keep asking her to tell me what's growing in it, but she seems to have lost interest. Oh, root it up, they're only weeds. She's had her chance.'

'But we gave it to her.'

'You're her parents, aren't you? You can take it back again. She can help with the veg, if she wants to. Promises get broken, sometimes. That's life, and she'll have to get used to it sooner or later.'

*   *   *

On the way home Sophia reflected on what she had said. 'Tough love' they called it these days, and it was true she'd never believed in mollycoddling. But it wasn't like her to be so callous when it came to Daisy. Surely she wasn't piqued by the failure of a nine-year-old girl to be interested in her silly flower bed project?

Or perhaps she was. And behind that was the uncomfortable knowledge that she was guilty of another betrayal, a bigger one. She wondered why Daisy hadn't told her mother that she sometimes let her play in the park by herself; it would have got her out of trouble that day at the flat, after all.

Sophia hadn't seen much of her granddaughter since then, although that could be for any number of reasons. It was silly to worry about it, she knew; Daisy was many things, but she wasn't a sulker. Yet she had to admit that she felt obscurely in the little girl's debt.

When she left the house Linda had given her a letter from Daisy, and now she decided to sit on the bench in the park and read it. Her granddaughter's childish phrases were just the thing to dissipate the cloud she was imagining had fallen over their friendship.

'*Dear Granny*,' the letter began. '*I do still love you but I don't want to write to you any more. Yours sincerely, Daisy.*'

*   *   *

It was nearly dawn the next day when they arrived in the little park, three of them, hoods up, pushing a scooter across the grass and under the trees.

The tallest one unscrewed the petrol cap and then set the scooter down on its side. Squatting down, he took something from his back pocket—a dishcloth? a headscarf?—and pushed it deep into the tank. Then, drawing it out a little way, he took a lighter and lit the end that hung out.

They stood back. When the fire reached the fuel there was a low *whump*, and the tank began to blaze. The plastic on the seat bubbled and melted, the foam inside it burning easily. One of them made a call, the phone disappearing inside his hood. They left unhurriedly.

The scooter burned slowly. At one point it looked like going out, but then one of the tyres caught fire and the flames sprung high again. As the sky lightened the flames seemed almost to disappear, though the air still wavered above them and the plume of black smoke became more distinct.

Then a soft rain began to fall, and by the time Sophia got up it was out. All that was left was a charred skeleton in the centre of a black and ashy pile, the buttercups and daisies curled and dead for feet around it, the ash tree's overhanging leaves reduced to grey cinders on blackened twigs.

18

ST SWITHIN'S DAY

All morning the old Jamaican man worked the traffic at the lights, a can of Red Stripe in one hand, the other knocking cheerfully at each window. He moved between the cars as though they could not touch him, and perhaps it was true. Every so often he retired to the pavement and sat in the hedge, talking unhurriedly to himself. The depression where he sat was permanent, and shaped like a throne. At around noon he ambled away up Glebe Road, his shadow short on the hot July pavement.

The weather was set fair, and every day Denny dared more soft furnishings outside the shop. On Dartmoor and Exmoor the close, springy turf was starred with yellow tormentil, while in Kent pink mallow dressed every roadside and the apples swelled like green knots in the orchards. From the cockpit of a Typhoon, tearing the wide skies of East Anglia on a training run from RAF Coningsby, the country which pitched and yawed below looked impossibly green.

*   *   *

Little seemed to be expected of TC at school, by anyone, and if it wasn't for the register he felt as though he could disappear and nobody would even notice. Mostly he just tried to come through each school day unchallenged and intact. In a week it would be the summer holidays, anyway; just a few more days, that was all, and then he would be free.

Now that the weather was warm and the days long he found he could stay out in the evenings until it was quite late. The common was often busy with people drinking or having barbecues, though, and the woods didn't really feel like his any more, not since the dog fight. Usually he just went to the secret garden instead.

Sleeping there that night had changed something, he didn't know what. When he had woken in a half-light full of dew and birdsong he'd felt somehow like an animal. Not in a bad way, not like when people called other people animals, which was stupid, considering how much worse people were; it was more that he'd felt . . . simpler, somehow; properly part of things, at last. All the other stuff didn't matter. It belonged to a different life.

He'd stayed there most of the next day; he hadn't wanted to leave. He knew there'd be hell to pay when he got home anyway, so he stayed away. It was that afternoon that he'd found something; something that made it all worth it—the dog fight, everything. Now he glowed with the secret. It made him feel invincible.

As soon as the holidays came he'd decided he was going to stay there every night. Then, he'd really be part of it: properly, like an animal. He'd invented a friend whose house he could be staying over at, if his mum were ever to ask. 'I'm going out to play with David,' he'd taken to saying. Mostly she didn't even look up from the telly.

He had started building a camp—a proper one, not just a hide. It wouldn't be fair to keep sleeping in the fox's den. He'd trampled the nettles in one corner of the garden and hauled bricks from under the ivy to make a floor. Then he'd broken some branches off the trees—not the oak, just the sycamores and some holly—and propped them up to make a shelter. The corner between the high wall and a fence protected the back of the camp, and he was hoping ivy would wend its way through the branches to make a roof, maybe even by next year. It wouldn't survive a really big downpour, but it was summer and the weather was nice anyway.

Sitting in it after school one day, his arms wrapped around his knees, he thought about what else he needed. He'd already brought some stuff from home—a jumper, a sheet, a fork, a loo roll, some tins of beans—the ones with the ring pulls— and cans of Coke, but he needed more things. He tried to think what his dad would have taken. What did they have in the army?

A knife was the best thing, a proper one, a sharp one. He thought of Jozef, and the wooden animals he made. He decided to ask the other man at the chicken shop, Musa, where Jozef lived; he wanted to talk to him properly, in private. There was another reason, too: he had something to give him, something in return for all the chess games, and the chips.

*　　　*　　　*

Fine new blades of grass were pushing up through the ash, but TC still didn't like looking at the burnt patch in the little park; it made him think of violence, and the circle of bloody grass under the oaks. Going past it he looked the other way. A song thrush insisted on the same four phrases from somewhere above him, again, then again.

Daisy was coming out of the estate with a man he didn't recognise. She looked sulky, but when she saw TC she tugged urgently at the man's hand, turned to ask him something and ran over.

'Hello! My daddy says I can play with you for five minutes. What d'you want to play?' she said. The man was going towards the benches, but TC could see that he was watching them closely.

'I can't.'

'Yes you can, course you can. Let's climb a tree. Bet I can do it better than you!'

'I can't, I'm busy.'

'What is it, is it a secret, can I come?'

'No!' he said, rounding on her. 'I already *said*!'

Daisy took a step back. 'What is it you've got in your pocket?'

'Nothing.'

'Show me!' She made a grab for his arm and TC wrenched it away, seeing Daisy's father stand up out of the corner of his eye.

'Just . . . leave me alone!' he shouted, and ran.

*   *   *

'He is at his new work,' said Musa. 'What you want, you want food?'

TC shook his head. 'I got something for him. D'you know where he lives?'

'He got a new place, on the high road. But he won't be there now. He'll be here tonight—late shift. From ten. You still be awake?'

TC nodded. 'I'll come back.'

'Eh, my kids they are in bed by nine,' Musa said, wiping the counter. 'You should do the same, kid.

185

You got a growing brain, you need your sleep.'

But he was talking to an empty shop.

* * *

Jozef was on the common, litter picking. There was only another half-hour until the end of the shift, and he wanted to finish the section he'd been given. There were lots of beer cans on the grass, and plastic bags tangled in the brambles along the fence.

He looked at his watch. It didn't do to look too keen—he had worked that out quite quickly. There were six in his team, and none of them would be doing it if they had another way of making money. Except me, he thought. I would do it, I want to do it.

They worked in pairs. Today he was with Chima, the blackest man he had ever seen. There was a Ukrainian, Nazariy, who the others all seemed to assume Jozef should have some kind of kinship with; in fact, they had very little in common, and it was Chima he preferred to work with. Nazariy was always joking around, but there was an edge to it, a challenge. Chima kept himself to himself; he had his earphones in most of the time. But when Jozef had hauled the cross out of the pond it was Chima who had come and looked at it, turning it over carefully in his hands. 'This is a bad business,' he had said softly. Jozef had wondered what it was that Chima was picturing.

Now they approached each other slowly along the fence, each with a bag and grabber. Jozef's right hand inside the work glove ached a little; hours of squeezing the handle took their toll, especially if you tried to get the fiddly things like cigarette butts,

186

which he did.

'Jozef. Jozef!' He looked up. Chima had taken his earphones out and was beckoning him urgently. 'Come see.'

Jozef hoped it wasn't anything awful. The men exchanged stories of the things they had found, and Jozef did not want to have a story of his own.

Chima was pointing at a tree. It was a black locust, a *grochodrzew*; it had finished flowering but was still hung with browning pennants. At first Jozef couldn't make out what he was supposed to be looking at, but then he saw it: among the leaves, at about head height, a huge, humming knot of bees.

The swarm was in perpetual motion, but the noise coming from it was only a low murmur, and few bees flew around it; most simply clung to their fellows, moving slightly. The body of the swarm was bigger than a football.

'*Kurwa,*' said Jozef under his breath. He still found it hard to swear in English; the words came out wrong, for some reason—either too forceful, or not enough.

Seeing that Jozef had seen the swarm, Chima backed away. 'What do we do?' he asked.

Jozef shrugged. 'Tell Frank.'

'You stay here, then. Keep people away.' Chima jogged off to find the foreman.

Jozef remembered the time Stefan Gruszka's bees had swarmed in the walnut tree near the farmhouse. His father fetched Stefan in the jeep while his sisters hid inside the house. When Stefan came he explained that the bees weren't angry, they were just seeking a new home; they wouldn't sting anyone unless they tried to hurt them. Even so, the

187

women would not come out of the house. Stefan made a fire in a jerrycan and smoked the bees; after a few moments they fell out of the tree into a canvas bag, and he took them home. 'Won't they just leave again?' Jozef had asked, and his father had explained that Stefan had a new hive ready for them, so that they could be nearby to pollinate the orchard and they could all have cider.

When Chima came back he had the rest of the crew with him. Frank had already radioed it in, and had received instructions to tape the area off until environmental health could get there.

'Environmental health?' asked Jozef.

'Yeah, they'll come and get rid of it. It's a pisser, really; we can't go off-shift until they come, in case some silly bugger gets stung.'

'The bees are not owned by anybody?'

'No, mate, not in a swarm, not if they've gone wild.'

'So they kill them?'

''Fraid so. Right, Chima, Stevo: back to the van for some warning tape and some posts. Six, I'd say. See if there's any Footpath Diversion signs while you're at it. Christ, I hope they don't fly off, it'll be a bugger to keep up.'

'How long until the health people come, boss?' That was Nazariy.

'Let's get it taped off, then we'll have a think about who needs to stay late, OK? Anyway, it's overtime, it's not like you won't get paid.'

Nazariy sat on the grass with Mo, the Bengali, and began to roll a cigarette. There were scorch marks from barbecues on the grass nearby, and Mo brushed at one critically. Jozef stood and considered the peaceable bees.

Frank's radio let out a crackle, and he unhitched it from his belt, turning as he did so to scan the park behind them.

Jozef moved forward. Stepping quietly through the long grass and nettles, he reached the swarm in a few paces. Behind him he heard Nazariy. 'Hey, Joe, what you doing? Boss! Boss!'

The bees were moving slowly. A few flew lazily around the dense swarm. Jozef took his right glove off and dropped it at his side.

'Oi, Jozef!' That was Frank. 'What in fuck d'you think you're doing?'

Jozef made his fingers into a kind of beak. He tried to hold his hand steady, but he could see that it shook slightly. Then he pushed it slowly into the mass of bees.

It was surprisingly warm inside the swarm. He felt the minute oscillation of thousands of wings and thousands of chitinous bodies against his scarred and calloused hand. He saw, vertiginously, that his hand had disappeared up to the wrist.

Inside the swarm he felt for the branch they were attached to. He moved his fingers slowly, slowly; the worst thing would be to crush one. One sting, he felt instinctively, would mean dozens.

He could hear the men's voices behind him, but they weren't important. What was important was to manoeuvre his fingers around the branch so as to gain enough purchase to snap it—and to snap it with as little movement or disturbance as possible. He realised he was holding his breath, and let it out slowly.

He looked at the twigs protruding from the swarm to see if the branch was bowing. If he could judge the weight of the swarm he could anticipate

189

any recoil. There was a bee flying around his eyes, and his eyebrows were gathering sweat.

Inside the swarm his fingers felt a fork in the twig and he used it to brace his thumb as he snapped. Immediately the hum of the bees increased in pitch; Jozef froze, holding the branch in the same place, willing the bees to settle.

After a moment he began to take slow steps back, the swarm a dark mass clenched around his fist. The men were shouting and swearing, but Jozef kept his eyes fixed on the bees.

Once he was out of the long grass he looked briefly left, to the oak woods. Few people went there, and it would be much easier to tape off. He wondered what would happen if, when he let go of the branch, the bees did not go with it.

He began to walk slowly across the common, the men keeping their distance behind.

'Chima,' he said quietly.

'Here.' Chima jogged up beside him, looking warily at the bees.

'Tell Frank I will put it down under the trees, far from the path. It will be better there. And can he send somebody ahead, clear a place, OK?'

'OK—but why are you doing this?'

'I know this kind of tree,' Jozef replied. 'The branches, they break easily. Very easily. It's better I break it myself, take the bees away.'

Chima fell back, and the men watched as Jozef advanced carefully across the grass. But when he was a hundred yards or so away the bees lifted, as one, from his outstretched fist and funnelled up into the empty sky.

It was as Jozef had hoped. He stood and watched them fade into the blue, a lone figure holding

190

a forked branch as though he would call down lightning from the summer sky.

*   *   *

TC took a cigarette packet from his pocket and put it on the takeaway counter. 'Go on,' he said, and grinned up at Jozef.

'You are sure?'

TC nodded, and Jozef flipped back the lid, shook something out into his palm. The back of his right hand was red and shiny, the knuckles almost lost in the swollen flesh.

'Owl pellets,' said TC. 'You know.'

Jozef nodded gravely. 'So this is what you have found. Can I know where?'

TC grinned again, glowed. 'The secret garden. It's a tawny; two. Do you believe me?'

Jozef nodded again. 'Of course. You know, this is very special. Very special. You are going to keep lookout?'

TC nodded.

'Have you told anyone?'

TC shook his head. 'D'you think I should?'

'Well . . .' Jozef paused for a moment. 'This is perhaps important, you know. It could be nobody knows there are these birds in the city. People will want to see where these birds are.'

He read the boy's open face. 'But perhaps . . . perhaps you can find out more first, like where is the nest, how many for sure. And holidays are coming, yes? So why don't you watch them for . . . say . . . one month, then we decide.'

He cupped the little agglomerations of bone and hair in his big hand and examined them closely,

191

then held his palm out to the boy, but TC picked out only one to return to the cigarette packet.

'You can borrow the other,' he said, 'if you want.'

'Thank you,' said Jozef, closing his hand around it carefully. 'I would like that very much.'

19

DOG DAYS

Across the country the sun was ripening the wheat, pouring down, drawing the ears up and turning them golden, like bread. In East Yorkshire and North Lincolnshire the pea harvest was coming in, destined for the Birds Eye plant.

As the sun climbed each day skylarks ascended from the fields and moors and hung above them, singing: thousands upon thousands of them, each alone, inviolate, but together a host, a choir. The nights were humid, and Sirius flickered like fire in the south-west.

At the start of the summer holidays all roads west were busy. Car after car thundered past the hazel and hawthorn scrub, loaded with luggage, bikes and dinghies. The traffic was a hot roar, the tarmac a mirage, but the motorway verges teemed with life: butterflies and beetles, mice, voles and rabbits; and the long grass between the low thickets and the lay-bys zithered with emerald grasshoppers.

*   *   *

In the city the day had dawned clear before resolving itself once more into heat. Sophia had found it difficult to sleep and was up early, watching the starlings through her kitchen window as they hunted the dry grass in packs, heads down. The nettles were spent and limp, the white trumpets of convolvulus like crumpled tissues in between; early blackberries were green knots among the brambles. Where the sun hit the desire paths the ground had hardened and fissured, dun-coloured. Dog walkers' and joggers' feet kicked up a dry mud as fine as dust which settled slowly behind them.

She sat at the kitchen table in her old cotton housecoat, the local paper before her, and waited for the palpitations to subside. It was like having a wild bird inside her chest, fluttering, fluttering. She sat perfectly still so that she would not tax it further. After a few moments it gave a twist, then a shudder, and seemed to stop altogether. Anxiously she held her wrist between thumb and finger; there, beneath the papery skin, twitched a faint but regular pulse, the motion of her heart in her chest as imperceptible as usual now its normal rhythm had returned.

She did not feel faint or sick, but she had started to feel frightened. Each time it happened it seemed to go on a little longer, although when she was hooked up to the monitor in the hospital her heart had refused to turn tricks, and so, it seemed, they would not treat it yet.

The paper was full of the usual horrors: the borough's women and children variously outraged, a little boy drowned while swimming in a canal, muggings, a rape. And the heat: the usual mixture of glee and complaint. The photos were of city types picnicking in the parched confines of urban squares, as though that was what summer meant.

She put it aside and thought about Daisy. She still saw her granddaughter, of course, but she missed the letters, and more than that she missed the secrets between them. Last time Daisy had visited she had insisted on doing her homework, and when Sophia had suggested she go and play outside Daisy had reminded her, archly, that she was not allowed.

Undermining her mother's authority wasn't right, though; Sophia could see that now. For a long while there had been a distance between her and Linda, and she had focused her attention on Daisy instead. The distance between her and her daughter had made it easy for her to pass judgement on Linda's decisions and priorities, easy to collude with the little girl in whose unconditional love she had so selfishly basked. Yet Linda was only trying to do the best for Daisy, just as she had for Linda and Michael, and things were clearly very different these days. She had no right to think that she knew better.

She opened the kitchen window for the breeze and went to run a cool bath. In the streets around the estate the buddleia was coming into bloom, and its fragrance rode into the empty room on a breath of monoxide and bins.

*   *   *

TC barely noticed the stink of the stairwell; like everyone else in the block he was used to it, and besides, he was thinking. Tonight was going to be his first proper night in his camp, and hopefully the first of many. At the back of his mind was a little thought that said maybe this was it: maybe he wouldn't have to go home again. He knew it probably wasn't true, but the summer holidays stretched infinitely ahead, far too long to see the end of. So he needed to think carefully about what he could take with him, in case she didn't come looking for him, in case this was his last ever time at home.

He wanted to take his duvet, but it was too bulky; there was a big orange towel, though, that would do for now. What else? The tin-opener would be good, and there was a candle in the bathroom. Some lighters. More food.

When he was there, nobody would be able to make him do anything. Nobody would even know where he was. Although—was that OK? It felt strange to think of that, that he would be alone and not even one grown-up would know where he was in the world. Should he tell someone, tell Jozef? But no, he was used to being by himself, he'd be OK. Wouldn't he?

As he let himself in with his key he heard music. His mum must be in. He froze, considered backing out, but it was too late.

'TC?'

He went in, shut the door behind him. 'Yeah.'

'In here.' She was on the couch—not just her—it was Jamal as well. Jamal.

'Eh, kid, how you doing?'

TC stared at them both. 'What's going on, Mum?'

'We—we got something to tell you.'

'You're back together.'

'Ain't you pleased?'

'When?'

'Doesn't matter when.'

'Thas all right'—that was Jamal. He grinned at TC, stuck out his hand. 'Come on, you must've missed my cooking, eh, kid?'

TC looked at his hand, looked around. The lounge was tidy, the windows open; it felt different, somehow. Why?

'Jamal's moving in, OK?' his mum said. So that was it. 'He's gonna live here.'

'With us?'

'Yeah with us. Who'd you think?'

TC knew he would say it; he couldn't help himself. 'But . . . what about Dad?'

'Your dad ain't coming back, OK? Jesus *fuck*, TC, you know that.'

TC looked at her face, the way it was turned away from him again. He had made that happen; he had done it by asking about his dad. He wanted her to look at him again, he wanted her to ask about him, where he'd been, or if he was hungry. Something.

'Sorry,' he said.

She breathed out. 'Fuck's sake.'

He looked at Jamal, wanted to say his name, but it got stuck somewhere. 'You're not my dad, though, OK?' he whispered.

'I know that, kid,' said Jamal, with a look TC couldn't interpret, 'believe me.'

*　　　*　　　*

They had been into his room and tidied it up. Clean sheets on the bed and his clothes all put away, even his socks in pairs. They had found the box he kept under his bed, and now his things were

196

all out on the windowsill: the Lego, the headless Luke Skywalker, the crow's skull, the stone with the hole and the half-pence piece. And his two books, leaning against the window embrasure: *The Paranormal*, with its chilling cover, and *A Guide to Tracking Wild Animals*. Even the jay's feather was there.

He sat down on the bed and looked at the wall and wondered what it was he was supposed to do.

*　　　*　　　*

'Look, Kel—'

'I know. I *know*, all right?'

They were in the kitchen, Jamal leaning on the table, Kelly with her back to him, staring into the open fridge.

'He's a good kid.'

She sighed. 'I'll speak to him. Later.'

'If this is going to work, Kel—'

'It's me you're fucking moving in with, Jamal, not him.'

'He lives here too, Kelly—at least, he should do. Can't blame him for not being around too much, though.'

'He's fine.'

'He ain't fine. Look, you can't just ignore him. He's your kid.'

'I ain't ignoring him, OK? Jesus, Jamal, what is this?'

Jamal reached around her and took a beer from the fridge, sat down at the kitchen table.

'Kel. He's your *kid*, OK? You gotta look after him a bit more.'

'I never wanted him in the first place! I was

nineteen, for fuck's sake, I didn't know any better.'

'Keep it down, yeah? And it's tough, anyway. He's here, and he needs you.'

'No he don't. He's never here except to eat, he never talks to me.'

'You never talk to him, either.'

'That's cos he only ever wants to talk about his dad.'

'Jesus, Kel, he's a little boy. He misses his dad. I can understand it. He don't know the guy beat you, he don't know why you split up.'

'It ain't his business, OK?' She pushed past him into the lounge, put the TV on. He followed her, shutting the door behind them.

'Kel, it *is* his business,' he hissed. 'You ain't being fair.'

'Life ain't fucking fair, Jamal, is it. What is it you want from me? He's got a home, food on the table.'

'And that's enough, is it?'

'It's all I fucking got from my mum. Look, Jamal, are you going to be on my case the whole time? Because if you are, this ain't gonna work out.'

'Don't you . . . love him?'

She let out a breath. 'Course I do.'

'Really? It don't look like that.'

And then she was crying. 'I did. I do. *Fuck*. I just can't . . .'

Jamal took the can gently from her hand and set it on the table, crouching down beside the sofa as she knuckled her eyes angrily. 'Listen, Kel. It ain't too late. It's the summer holidays now, yeah? Why don't you think of some things you can do together, you and TC? Don't have to be much. You just need to spend some time with him, OK? He ain't his dad; he's a good kid. You just forgot.'

198

Jozef was whittling again, a gift for the boy. He stood at the bedsit's window with his knife and worked slowly. It was nearly finished, but to rush now would be fatal. It was so easy to let the blade slip at the end, just when you thought the job was done and stopped paying attention.

He put the carving down and fed Znajda in the kitchen, standing and watching as she pushed the bowl around the kitchen floor. Even when there was nothing left, nothing at all, still she kept at it, her pink tongue edging the plastic bowl along the skirting board. Finally she came to stand by his leg and looked up at him, her body wagging gently.

Her bowls had been among the first things he had bought for the new place. The other bits he got from the market and a trip to Ikea in Emir's van; the landlord had contributed an old cathode ray TV and a mattress. He could have done with some bits and pieces from the clearance shop, but he hadn't been that way in weeks.

He had surprised himself with how quickly he had settled in. The first time he took Znajda there she had refused the staircase outside, looking dubiously at its metal treads. But when Jozef called her from the top she had barrelled gamely up it, calling from it a paroxysm of joyous clangs. Once inside she sniffed the worn blue carpet carefully before seeking out the only shaft of sun and lying down in it.

Now she had a folded blanket to sleep on; from it she could see the whole bedsit, so Jozef was never out of her sight. Even when she seemed most deeply asleep, flat out and gently snoring or yipping and twitching after dream-squirrels, even then she would open a rolling eye the moment he stirred. Looking at her at such times Jozef found it hard to remember that at one time he had thought her ugly and brutish. He wondered what had been the matter with him.

He loved having Znajda there, but he was aware that beyond her was a loneliness she could only go a little way towards shoring up. Apart from TC, Musa was the closest he had to a friend, but although they got on he didn't need Jozef, and Jozef knew little of his life away from the takeaway. Working in the parks Jozef mostly kept himself to himself; they all did. The turnover was high, Chima and Nazariy already gone. It felt like a long time since he had been important to anybody. The boy, perhaps; but that was something he had to be careful about, he knew.

And there was more, of course. He missed home all the time, and having his own place felt like staking a claim here, away from Poland, however impermanent the current arrangement could turn out to be. There was a betrayal in it somewhere, he couldn't help but feel.

He wrote to his mother, care of his youngest sister in Nowy Sacz; it was only his second letter since arriving in the country three years before. '*I am renting a little flat,*' he wrote. '*I have a dog. You would like her, she reminds me of Boska, do you remember Boska, Bernard's dog?*'

He wrote, '*I work outside now in the daytimes. I like it much better. It is very hot this year, much hotter than Poland, and I would not like to be inside all the time.*'

He did not write, *'Will you come and visit me?'*—not yet. He did not say that he would save up and come home at Christmas. He printed his new address carefully at the end and wondered if anyone would reply.

*   *   *

He was on his way back from the post office when he saw Denny. It was too late to change direction, and the smaller man had already seen him anyway. He was glad he did not have Znajda with him; unlike in Poland he'd found they did not welcome dogs in shops here, and he did not like to leave her tied up on the pavement.

'Oi, Joe,' Denny shouted from a few yards off, chin up, eyes squinting against the sun. 'Oi!' He let out a brief and piercing whistle, as though Jozef had not already acknowledged him, or as though he were a recalcitrant dog himself.

Jozef stopped, nodded at him. 'Denny. Are you well?'

'Am I well? Never mind if I'm fucking well. I hear you've got my dog.'

'It's true.'

'Going to bring it back, were you?'

'No, I don't think so.'

'You don't think so. *You don't think so.* And why don't you think so? It's my fucking dog, or am I missing something?'

'Denny . . .' Jozef made a calming gesture with both hands.

'You think I'm not fit, is it? Cos that's what I've heard.'

A group of white kids eating ribs at the bus stop

201

were grinning and staring, hopeful of a fight. One was aiming a cameraphone at them already.

'Denny, she—'

'It's my dog. I make good money off it. You know what I make off it?' He didn't wait for an answer. 'A ton each, maybe more. Five puppies, say, that's five hundred quid.'

'You want me to buy her.'

'Compensation, let's call it. And I'm doing you a fucking favour, as it goes. I could easily ask for more. You could make it back if you were smart, bred from it again. But you won't do that, will you? You're a soft cunt, is what it is. So. You bring it to the shop, yeah? Tomorrow. Or the dog. One or the other.' He walked on, past Jozef, calling, 'One or the other, OK?'

* * *

Later that afternoon Jozef took Znajda to the common. She stayed close, sensing his mood; when he sat down on the parched grass she subsided beside him, sniffing the air but content to stay there with his broad hand on her flank.

Jozef knew what he was going to do about Denny, and there was no sense in going over it. He let his mind drift back to the boy again, as it tended to do. He wanted to see him, maybe play a game of chess or take him to the cafe, maybe let him try some of his beer. He wanted to talk to him, tell him about Poland, ask him about the owls and the other creatures he'd found. He wondered how he could find him; maybe he'd call into the takeaway on the way back, see if he'd been in; maybe he'd have a look for him in the little park. The kid wanted to learn to use a knife; well, perhaps it was OK after all.

He thought about the first thing he'd whittled, and how it had felt to finish it: a crude bird that stayed on his father's dresser for years, even after his carvings became much more detailed and refined. Where was it now? he wondered. And what about the other things that had lived on the dresser: he had his father's knife, but where now was his pipe and his bone-handled comb? When you're gone, what happens to all the infinite, familiar things that make up your life?

The city sweltered, broiled, flickered like a mirage. Everything sounded sharp and off-key; everything felt either sticky or too dry. And the birds, who had been so voluble all spring while they had nests and mates and territories to defend—finally, now, the birds had fallen silent.

Znajda's brindled coat had grown hot under Jozef's hand. He got up and led her into the shade.

20

LAMMAS

For the first time that summer the Perseids darted like tracer fire, faint and intermittent, above the city all night. When the sky eventually lightened it revealed dew, heavy on the dry, dead grass of the little park. The blades hung, jewelled and still and briefly silver, draped between with a thousand tiny webs that caught and held the dew as a jeweller's cloth does diamonds. Then, as the sun rose above the roofs of the Plestor Estate and the dawn sky slowly deepened to blue, the light illumined the grey-veiled grass, and within ten minutes or so it was dry.

TC was at the top of the fire escape when Jozef left his flat. He opened the door and there he was, one foot frozen on the highest tread, a khaki kitbag far too big for him hooked around one skinny shoulder.

'I—I—the man at the takeaway said—'

'It's OK. Come in. Everything is OK?'

'Were you off out?'

'In a moment, yes. But it can wait a little bit. Come, come.'

He took the bag from the boy and followed him into the flat, closing the door behind them both. Znajda came and looked up at TC, flipping her ears back for a stroke.

'Big bag,' Jozef said, and swung it onto the chair. 'You are going somewhere?'

'Not really. Sort of.'

'You want to tell me?'

'Just to the secret garden. You know, the place I told you about. Not running away, just—just—I've got a camp. I thought I could stay there. But I don't know if I've got all the right stuff. I mean, I think I have. Not forever, just the holidays. I thought—I thought . . .'

Sometimes, Jozef thought, you don't know what it is you really want from people. What you ask for isn't always what you need.

'You want to borrow something?'

'A knife. I mean, your knife. Or if you had another. I'll give it back, I promise.'

Jozef went to the open window and looked at the

204

buses passing on the high road below. He couldn't give the boy a knife, and he couldn't let him run away to sleep rough in some godforsaken corner of the city, but to refuse him now would be to lose his trust—and who else was there to look out for him?

He turned back and folded his arms. 'I am hungry. You hungry?'

TC nodded.

'OK. I will go out and get breakfast. We eat, then we go through your things, find out if you have everything you will need. You like eggs? Good. And some ham, I think.' Jozef switched on the TV. 'Is not very good, only five channels. But here is the control. Now, you stay here, OK? I go to the shop, but I have—I have something else I have to do first. It won't take long, though. I will be maybe fifteen, twenty minutes, OK?'

*   *   *

The sound of Jozef's feet on the metal stairs faded away, and TC sat down on the chair. He patted his legs to call Znajda over, but she wouldn't budge from the door. She had really wanted to go with Jozef; he'd had to push her gently back inside when he pulled the door to, and she had cried a little bit, which wasn't like her. Now she lay by the door with her head between her paws.

The bedsit was small, but it was so neat and tidy, so . . . cosy, or something. TC got up and went into the kitchen: there were three new tea towels folded on top of the fridge, and the hob was spotless. An old jar held a wooden spoon, a paring knife and a tin-opener; he picked up the knife and looked at it, but put it back. In the corner of the kitchen were

205

Znajda's two bowls on a plastic mat; something about seeing them there made TC feel nice inside.

In the main room the TV laughed and chattered: kids' programmes. TC flicked it off with the remote. Into the silence came the sound of the traffic rumbling past, and he drifted over to the window to look out.

On the sill was a little carving, an owl with fierce eyes and feathers that looked somehow soft, despite the wood; and TC knew that it was meant for him. He picked it up and examined it; it felt warm, and fitted so exactly into his palm. Without thinking he slipped it into his pocket.

He looked around the room. It would be so brilliant to have somewhere that was just yours; it would be almost better than the camp. But the camp was still good, he thought. He could watch over the owls there, and besides, this was Jozef's place, not his, and the camp would be his, with his things in it. As long as the weather stayed nice it would be OK. And Jozef would help him, Jozef was really nice, he hadn't told him off about it or anything. It wasn't weird or anything that they were friends. Maybe he would tell Jozef where the camp was after all. Just so somebody knew. Just in case.

There was a black-and-white photograph Blu-tacked to one wall, and TC went over to look at it, sitting carefully on the edge of the neatly made bed. It showed a family outside a house with a wooden porch. The mother and father sat on chairs, the mother with a baby in her arms, and around them stood four children. They all looked old-fashioned; not just because of the black-and-white picture—there was something else, but TC wasn't sure what it was. The clothes weren't too

206

olden-day, although the mother wore a headscarf; maybe that was it. And their faces—they didn't look like anyone he knew, anyone from the city. They looked . . . long gone, somehow. Or far away, perhaps; and perhaps it was the same thing.

A girl of about four, TC guessed, stood slightly awkwardly with one hand on her mother's shoulder; it looked as though she had just been told off for fidgeting. Another girl, a bit older, stood on the right, and behind the seated parents were the two tallest children, a girl and a boy. The boy was squinting into the light, and his hair was all messy and big. TC realised with a start that it was Jozef.

Znajda heaved a sigh and raised her eyes balefully to TC. Perhaps she needed to go to the toilet, he thought; she had really wanted to go out with Jozef before, and now she was just lying by the front door as though she was trying to tell him something. What if she peed on the carpet, would it be his fault? Jozef hadn't said anything about that, but maybe it was supposed to be obvious. He'd never been in charge of a dog by himself before; there was probably stuff everybody knew except him.

When he stood up she raised her head and the stump of her tail moved hopefully. He decided to take her across the road to the little park; from the benches he'd be able to see the entrance to the laneway behind the shops, and could keep an eye out for Jozef when he came back.

Leaving the flat with Znajda and his kitbag, he paused. The bag was far too heavy to cart about. He put it neatly away behind the flat door and swung it shut behind him.

Jozef arrived at the second-hand furniture shop as Denny was carrying an old hatstand out to the pavement. It rested on the smaller man's shoulder like a lance, its blunt hooks pointing towards Jozef, whose heart gave a dull chime and then was still.

'Well, well, well,' Denny said, putting the hatstand down beside a pair of armchairs and dusting off his hands. 'No dog, I see. You must have something for me.'

'Shall we go inside?'

'No, mate, I'm fine here.' He folded his arms. 'Got my money, then, have you?'

'Denny, I am not giving you any money for the dog.'

'Oh, is it. Is it really. Well, well. And no dog either. You must think I'm a cunt.'

'I think you were right yesterday. You . . . you are not fit.'

'I'm not fit? *I'm not fucking fit?*' Denny's face flushed, but he looked calm and almost joyful in his self-righteousness and rage. He began walking slowly towards Jozef, who held his ground. 'Who the *fuck* are you, *fucking Polack*,' he enunciated very precisely, 'to tell me that I am not *fucking fit?*'

As he reached Jozef he sprang up in a small movement, fists clenched but held by his sides. His head cracked Jozef's nose with stunning force, and Jozef felt the pavement rush up to meet him behind.

Denny stood over him and grinned. A small crowd had formed, but at a distance. 'You're a fucking poof, Joe, you know that?' he said. 'A fucking, horrible poof.'

Jozef got up, slowly, and looked levelly at Denny. He could feel the weight of his father's knife in his jeans pocket, but put the thought away. He touched the back of his hand to his nose, gently, and saw it come away red.

'You can have that one,' he said. 'But here is what I got to say. You tell the council about everything you find in the houses, Denny? You write it all down properly, what is there, anything of value? You never sell something on the side, don't write it down, don't give the money to the council, the relatives? Don't forget, I worked with you for over one year. I was there at the houses, after someone die. I see what you do, Denny. So. You want to talk about my dog some more, you come and see me. You come and see me any time.'

*   *   *

He forgot the breakfast stuff. It didn't matter anyway. He wondered what he should say to TC about what had happened. He could feel both his eyes swelling shut.

Years since he'd had a fight; *years*. Kraków, probably. Not that this was one, not really. He'd known what Denny would want, what it would require, and he had not intended to fight back unless he had to. The headbutt, though, that had been a shock; he'd pictured a punch, forgotten Denny's height, and his own. What a strange thing violence was, both petty and shocking at the same time. The blood on the stones; the spectre of what could have happened crowding around them on the pavement as the buses rumbled past. He was proud of himself for walking away.

Now he was full of adrenalin, buzzing with it. He felt ready for anything, but strangely ardent, too. He wanted to go home and see Znajda, make sure she was safe; he felt a rush of tenderness for her. And the boy, too; it seemed clear, now, that he should just tell him not to run away where he couldn't find him, that he should find a way to help him, somehow, himself. Perhaps it really could be that simple; perhaps he had been worrying too much before.

He took the stairs two at a time—but the flat, when he opened the door, was empty. He stood in the doorway, his key still in the lock. No kitbag on the chair, either: fuck, he thought, this time in English; *fuck*. The boy had gone to wherever it was he was hiding out, and he'd taken Znajda. He should have stayed, talked to him. But he'd had this thing hanging over him, and he'd wanted a chance to think. Now he'd lost it—the chance, and the boy. *Fuck*.

Jozef clanged back down the stairs and jogged out onto the high road, sweat gathering above his eyes and in the small of his back. The sun blazed above, and the hot city stank. *Think. Think.* Maybe the old lady would know; she saw all the comings and goings from the window of her flat. He dodged between the traffic and headed towards the little park.

* * *

On her way back from dropping Daisy at her mother's, Linda walked into an atmosphere as thick and febrile as kerosene. A group of people had gathered on the pavement, aimlessly loitering with hands in pockets but with none of the defeated demeanour that marks those waiting for a bus. They looked keyed up, somehow—although this information came in well under Linda's radar. She looked around, but apart from a small, chippy-looking man disappearing into the junk shop, there was nothing to see. Still, she clamped her bag a little closer under her arm and picked up her pace as she walked on.

She had only witnessed a fight once, and it had been an unedifying affair. None of the *biff!* and *pow!* of the movies; it was all grabbing and shoving, and over very fast. It was the summer after she left school and she had been, what, sixteen?

I knew nothing, *nothing*, she thought. But I thought I knew everything. That was the really dangerous age, and she dreaded it with Daisy. The world was changing even faster now, faster than it had between her mother's youth and her own, and who knew what Daisy would have to confront that she had no hope of understanding.

Before she'd even got her O-level results she'd rejected the idea of university, although she knew it broke both her parents' hearts. But she wasn't quite ready for the world yet, either. She'd wanted one last summer holiday before the rest of her life began, and with that huge unknown drawing closer day by day she'd discovered in herself a vein of recklessness, a nose for danger, that she'd never acknowledged before—and hadn't since.

Never again, she thought now. It had been a bit like being subtly possessed; a delicate slew rather than a full-on career, but a state in which she heard herself say yes to things before her brain had had a chance to raise its usual objections. Yes

211

to gig tickets, yes to cider, yes to kitten heels and cigarettes. And yes to boys.

She'd lost her virginity that summer, of course. Like a skin to be shed, it was something to get over with before her real life—as she had thought of it then—began.

'Horrible, horrible,' she found herself muttering now, shaking her head slightly to be rid of the memory. As for the fight, she could barely remember how it had started. The boy she had slept with and . . . who was it? God, what time did to you. He must have been someone she knew well, back then, but damned if there was anything left of him now.

Yet the fight itself was like yesterday. They had been hanging about in the park, her and her friends, when it kicked off. She had stood up as the boys scuffled, her heart racing in joy and horror—and suddenly there was her dad, weighing in from nowhere, as angry as she had ever seen him. He pulled the lads apart as though they were children, told them to get lost. And then he had looked at her there by the bench, in her short skirt and frosted pink lipstick, and she had hung her head.

Later that day, when she had finally slunk back to the flat, she had wondered what she was in for. But nothing was ever mentioned, and if her mother knew, she never said anything about it.

*　　　*　　　*

TC was about to go back to Jozef's when Znajda took off. One moment she was beside him; the next she was streaking out of the park towards the busy traffic. TC raced after her, shouting her name, but

212

she was like a bullet. She barrelled into Jozef as he turned off the high road onto the grass, jumping and crying and trying to lick his face. He crouched down to soothe her as TC caught up.

'There you are! I was looking for you—you were not at the flat. I thought you had run away, I thought I would not be able to find you.'

'Sorry—sorry—are you OK? What happened?'

'Is nothing. I am glad to find you. Get off, stupid dog.'

'She knew you were coming—she ran off to find you!'

'She is my good girl, my sweet girl,' he crooned. 'She has been worried about me, I can see.'

'Yeah—she just lay by the door, she must've wanted to go outside and find you. Are you OK? What happened?'

'And I wanted to find you. Come, let's sit down for a moment,' he said, nodding towards the benches and the shade. 'I need to get my breath.'

*   *   *

'TC's talking to a bad man.'

Daisy, who had not helped with the cake mix and who did not actually care what kind of icing it should have, was looking out of Sophia's kitchen window.

'What's that, sweet pea?'

'TC. You know, TC. He's talking to a bad man.'

'What bad man? Where?' Sophia peered through the glass. 'No he isn't, that's Jozef. He's perfectly nice. You can't go round thinking everyone's a bad man, Daisy, it's ridiculous.'

'He isn't nice, he's a bad man. Look, he's got

blood on him.'

'I'm sure he hasn't. Now come on, madam, I need you to stir the mixture, or you can't lick the bowl afterwards.'

'He looks like a—like a *pikey* to me. And he's got a horrible dog.'

'*Daisy!* What did you just say?'

Daisy had known the word was bad when she said it. She had said it anyway; she had made her granny angry on purpose. Now she coloured. 'Nothing.'

'Yes you did, young lady. I heard you quite clearly. Now you listen to me,' Sophia said, taking her granddaughter by the shoulders. 'Jozef is *not* a bad man, and he is not a pikey. And don't you dare use that word again, d'you hear me? *Ever*. Not in this house.'

Daisy squirmed out of her grasp, suddenly furious. 'Mummy says pikey, so there, and there *are* bad men, whatever you say. People are *always* getting killed, *always*. You just never watch TV, so you don't know. You think you know everything, but you don't. You're just a—just a stupid old woman with romantic ideas!'

'That's not true,' said Sophia, putting her hand to her chest where her heart was skipping and lurching. The words were clearly Linda's, and she felt her eyes fill with tears that she tried to blink away. 'That's just not true!'

'Yes it is. Yes it is! If there aren't bad men then why aren't I allowed to play by myself?'

'Because—because your mother says so.'

'You didn't used to care what she said! You never cared before! You let me, and I could have got kidnapped or—or killed. Just like TC is now!

214

And you don't even care!'

Sophia sat down at the table. The pain in her chest was new; an ache. She breathed carefully and tried not to feel frightened.

'I'm going out there right now,' Daisy said, marching towards the door. 'I'm going to—to spy on the bad man and save TC. You can even tell Mummy, I don't care.'

She left the door open behind her and Sophia knew she wanted her to follow. In just a moment, she thought, when my heart stops, when I can get my breath. Just a moment. And until then, I can see her from here.

* * *

'Were you in a fight?'

'It's nothing. A man—I used to work for him. He doesn't like me.'

'Why not?' TC seemed jumpy and upset by the aftermath of violence.

'He . . . he doesn't like people like me.'

'Polish people?'

'Yes, perhaps. And he wants money, and I did not want to give it to him. It doesn't matter, you know? It is over. *Koniec*. Everyone OK.'

'Does it hurt?'

'A little. Not so much now. My nose—I have broken it before. So who knows, maybe this will make it better, what do you think? Maybe it will make me a handsome man.' Jozef smiled, but carefully, and TC could see that it hurt.

'Now, we talk about you, eh? To be truthful, TC, I do not want you to run away.'

'I'm not running away. I told you, it's a camp,

215

and it's not like it's far.'

'The city—you know, it is not always a nice place for a young boy. You might not be safe.'

'It's nicer than home. And anyway, the secret garden *is* safe. It's secret, that's the whole point. And I'm by myself all the time anyway, it's not any different. Don't you think I can look after myself?'

'I know you can, of course. But what about your mother? She will worry about you if you don't come home, of course. Then what happens?'

'She doesn't care. I *told* you that.' TC looked down. 'I—I thought you understood. The garden—it's mine, it really is. I just want to be part of it, like the owls are. Properly, not just a visitor. And it's not like you can make things any better at home, is it?'

Jozef put his head in his hands and listened to the traffic roar like the sound of his own blood in his ears. He did understand; of course he did. At the same time it was madness. The boy had to have a home, a proper one. He couldn't live on a bit of waste ground, even in summer, even with Jozef's help; he was ten years old, *na miłość boską*. And yet the park, the common and the secret garden made up a beloved territory of a kind that Jozef recognised only too well. It was the richest, most stable thing in TC's life, and Jozef knew that if he were to summon the authorities it would mean tearing the child away from everything he really loved, and who was he to inflict that on him?

Jozef wished he had some experience of children. He wished he knew what the right thing to do was.

'What about your—your father?' he asked, stumbling slightly over the word.

TC stared ahead. 'He isn't—I haven't got one.'

216

The bilious notes of an ice-cream van drifted from a couple of streets away. The city air lay around them, exhausted and still.

After a moment TC took the wooden owl from his pocket and held it out to Jozef. 'I found this, at your flat. I'm sorry, I didn't mean to take it.'

Jozef smiled. 'That's OK. It was for you, anyway. A present.'

'Thank you, it's brilliant.' The boy smiled, but it was a small smile.

'You know what, though,' Jozef said, taking it from him and turning it in his hands, 'it's not finished. Come, I'll finish it now. You can watch, see how I do it, OK?'

He took the knife from his pocket and unsheathed it. Behind the benches, deep in the ivy, Daisy watched as the pitiless sun caught the blade.

*   *   *

Fourteen years since the row of limes had first been brutally pollarded, and yet still the shade they cast was very slight. Before long it had inched away from the benches where TC and Jozef sat; then the sun bore down on them and drove them to move.

'What if I show you it?' said TC, as they walked towards the road. 'Then you'll know it's safe.'

'Really? Your camp?'

'Yeah. You can see the owls, too. If you want.'

It was something; it was definitely something. And maybe later he could ask the old lady what to do. 'OK,' he said.

At the exit to the little park, Daisy, following fifty paces or so behind, paused. She looked back, but with the sun in her eyes it was impossible to tell

217

whether or not her grandmother was at the kitchen window.

TC and the man were walking side by side, the dog at the man's heel. She followed them into Curtilage Street, where they turned into a narrow alley. She waited on the pavement for a slow count of ten, then looked carefully round the corner.

The alley was almost choked with weeds and litter. At the end were some bins—and the dog, which lay in the shade and regarded her with level eyes. There was no sign of the man with the knife, or the boy.

She turned and ran.

*   *   *

'I'm going to call your grandmother. This is outrageous. *Outrageous!*' Linda paced about the kitchen, one hand on the back of her neck, while Steven leaned in the doorway, his arms folded. 'I knew it. I bloody knew it! She's irresponsible! She's not to be trusted!'

Daisy sat at the kitchen table. She had stopped crying, though she was still flushed, and now wore a mulish expression. 'You ask her,' she said. 'I don't care. She let me—she always lets me.'

Linda stared at her daughter for a moment. 'I will. But you'd better be telling the truth, young lady.' She picked up the phone and dialled, turning her back on them both while she waited for Sophia to pick up. Behind her the kitchen hung, airless and silent, for a long moment.

'No answer.' Linda turned back and put the phone on the table. 'She's probably gone out to look for Daisy. Steven, go out and find her, will you, let her know Daisy's OK? I can't face it.'

'In a second, love,' he said. 'Daisy, what was the other thing you said? About the man?'

'I told you, a bad man, I saw him with my friend. That's why I went outside.'

'What friend?' asked Linda.

'TC. You know,' Daisy said, appealing to her dad, 'you saw him that time. In the park.'

'Hold on,' said Linda. '*Who?*'

'A little boy Daisy knows,' said Steven. 'About her age, I think.'

'Where from? Which school?'

'No—he lives around here. Look—what were you saying, Daisy? What man?'

'A bad man, with one of those horrible dogs. He took TC away, that's why I followed them.'

Steven crouched down in front of her. 'Daisy. This is really, really important. You're not in any trouble, but you have to tell me the truth, OK? Now, what happened to the little boy?'

'He—he—' She looked from one parent to the other. It wasn't about Granny any more, and that was a relief, because it wasn't really Granny's fault, she knew that. They had just been cross with each other, which happened sometimes. But they loved each other really.

Her mummy and daddy were still staring at her; they *wanted* her to say it, there was no going back. And anyway, it was true.

'I saw a man with one of those horrible dogs, and a knife,' she said. 'He had blood on his clothes. He took TC down an alley and they disappeared.'

Steven picked up the phone and called the police.

219

21
ST BARTHOLOMEW'S DAY

the interview with social services was nearly over. It was the last in a long series—three weeks it had been, on and off. First the police, again and again; now the social. TC had been seen twice before this, by different case workers; they didn't seem to be able to decide whose responsibility he was. He had answered the same questions over and over, talked about it all so many times, sometimes with his mum there in the room, sometimes just with a copper and the social. He wondered, when they had finished asking questions, what they would do with him. He wondered what they had done with Jozef.

They kept on asking him, asking him. How had Jozef 'first approached' him, why he had let him buy him chips. Whether he had given TC any money or any presents. They'd taken the wooden owl away, and TC didn't know if he was allowed to ask for it back.

They wanted to know all about his bag. The coppers had found it when they searched Jozef's place and they wanted to know why it was there, they kept going on about it. TC knew he wasn't giving them the right answers; they kept looking at each other, and even though he could tell they were trying not to be nasty or frightening, because of him being a kid, even then he'd still cried, his mum looking at him in a way he didn't understand. He hadn't known—he still didn't know—what the right answers were.

It was the worst thing ever, when the coppers came for them. He'd been in the camp with Jozef, under the old pollard oak. Just sitting, quietly, the shade cool and quiet, the owls somewhere invisible above. They weren't saying much, just looking and drinking in the old garden and each thinking their separate thoughts.

It felt OK; Jozef was nice to have with him in the garden. When they dropped down from the fence he'd just stood still for a bit, he hadn't asked, 'Is this it?' or anything. He'd let TC lead the way along a little trail he'd made through the undergrowth, slowly, quietly, looking carefully around him. When they reached the camp he'd stopped, and TC, cross-legged on the bricks, had grinned up at him and said he could come in.

Jozef had asked him quietly about the owls, and TC showed him, pointing carefully up to the hole in the larch where the chicks were nearly ready to fledge. And there, on a branch against the trunk, was one of the parents, its stippled feathers nearly invisible against the bark. Jozef smiled at him then, his eyes shining, and TC had felt, at that moment, that it was brilliant having him there, that nothing had been lost by sharing the garden, nothing taken away. It was lovely.

Then the coppers had crashed in, shouting. They smashed the fence down, breaking and splintering it, crushing the vetch and the honesty and the morning glory under their big black boots. The light poured in through the terrible gap, the policemen poured in, they trampled the blackberries, nearly ripe, and the herb robert and nettles and everything that lived beneath, everything that scurried or crept and hadn't meant any harm. Jozef had stood up

221

when the fence came down; he stepped forward while TC cowered back. He stood and sheltered TC, and the coppers shouted and shouted at him, *Drop the knife! Drop the knife!* like he was a maniac or something. They grabbed Jozef and twisted his arms back, and TC couldn't help it, he turned and hid his face.

Then one of the coppers came and crouched over him and said his name, his proper name, and he looked past the copper and saw Jozef struggling, struggling, craning back over his shoulder as they dragged him away through the ivy and the long grass. And Jozef had smiled at him then, he'd tried to smile, and his eyes as they took him away said: *Don't worry, I'll be OK.* But TC didn't think that it was true.

*   *   *

The swifts had gone, and the skies above the city were blank and empty once more. No more wheeling sickles, no more rooftop dogfights, no more screams. Above the Children and Young Persons' Unit equinoctial clouds were gathering; it was still muggy, still summer, but the holidays were nearly over and Year Six, for TC, would start in just over a week.

'OK, TC, I think we've finished here.' The social worker lady began putting her bits of paper back in the folder and looking for her briefcase. 'Is there anything you'd like to ask before you go?'

TC looked down. Was he allowed? He wasn't sure. He felt the blood rush to his face.

'Is—is—do you know what happened to Jozef?'

'Mr Łopata has been released.'

222

'Because he didn't do anything?'

'That's all I can tell you, TC. He is no longer in police custody.'

There was so much TC wanted to tell them about Jozef, but they didn't want to hear it, not the police, and not the social either. That they were friends, that they cared about each other. That they were the same, somehow: lost. At least TC still had his wild places, though, at least the owls would still be there; Jozef had nothing, not his farm, not TC, not even Znajda any more.

TC's eyes pricked at the thought, and he decided to be brave. Not much else could happen to him, he felt, and he owed it to Jozef to try. 'Can I go and see him?' he asked.

'TC—' The social worker's eyes flicked over to TC's mum for a moment. 'TC, I don't think that would be a good idea. Anyway, you won't be here for long, it might be best to put it all behind you, OK, love?'

'What do you mean? Why won't I be here?'

His mum got up from the sofa, fiddled in her pockets for her fags. 'Your dad's taking you,' she said. 'They got in touch with him. I meant to say before.'

'I'm going to live with my dad?'

'That's right. Ain't you pleased?'

'TC—' that was the social worker, butting in with a stern look over TC's head at his mum—'TC, *I am* sorry; I had thought this had already been discussed. Your mum thought—*we* thought you might like to stay with your father for a while, maybe forever, if you want. It's a way away, of course, but he's got a room ready for you, and there's a school nearby. You'll be assigned a case

223

worker in his district who'll help you settle in, of course, but he says he's happy to have you, and we do always feel that if we can keep a family together—or partly together—then that's the best thing for yourself. What do you think, TC, do you want to go and live with your dad?'

TC looked over at Kelly, but she wouldn't meet his eyes. 'OK,' he whispered.

*   *   *

That evening dusk drew slowly down, lilac and blue, over the little park with its lone ash tree, over the secret garden and the Plestor Estate and the rows of terraced houses winking with yellow lights, as the city's gradual tilt on the earth's grand axis bore it slowly towards the outer dark. The hedges were populous with sparrows, fat with sleep but vaguely quarrelsome still, while above the common, starlings massed and wheeled and bore down on their ancient roosts.

Linda, at the villa on Leasow Road, was closing the curtains, shutting out the city with its noise and its dirt and its dangers. She moved from room to room, pulling the good drapes gently, moving them carefully into place. 'Glass of wine, love?' called Steven from the bright kitchen, as Daisy and Susannah giggled and squealed upstairs. 'That would be lovely,' she replied, turning her back on the darkening sky and taking her place at the computer, where, lit by its harsh blue glare, she typed in 'gardening services', then her postcode, and hit return. 'Wine is exactly what I need.'

Sophia watched the light fade from her hospital bed. She was wired up to machines, surrounded by them, and all she could see of the sky was a blank square, bereft even of a star this early in the night. She watched it slowly darken, and wondered at how far away the world felt, and how small she was, and frail. The table by her bed was covered in cards, and Linda came every day, but she knew that really, now, she was on her own.

At last the sky was black. The hospital was like a ship, she imagined, blazing with light, sailing away with her on board and leaving the teeming city behind.

Jozef was at the bus stop, a battered holdall in his hand and a wooden chess piece shaped like a dog in his jacket pocket. Where was Znajda now? he wondered. Where was his lovely girl, his sweet girl? It was almost too much to bear.

They had said she was a dangerous breed, they'd snared her around the neck with a catchpole and dragged her, choking, to the van. They'd pushed her into a cramped cage in the back and he had heard her crying, desperately, as he tried to explain about her, how she was a good girl, how they had rescued each other, how she was only protecting him. But they didn't want to know.

He'd asked around, after his release, about what would happen to Znajda—if she turned out to be the breed they'd said she was, if her head was a certain shape and size. It was obscene. He held the little carving tight and swung the holdall onto his shoulder as the bus drew up. How many buses would it take to forget the dog? he wondered, how many more for the boy? How far would he have to go to leave all this behind?

At last, it was fully dark. A car sped north on the motorway, one among many, dancehall on the radio

225

and the stink of fags seeping from the upholstery. From the front seat a small boy watched as the landscape around him faded into featureless dark, until he could see nothing ahead of him at all, only night. On the back seat a PlayStation, nearly new, shifted and slid, shifted and slid.

Above the road hung an invisible legion of thunderheads, massed and angry in the night sky and heavy with a whole summer's rain. A drop pelted the windscreen, a dozen, a hundred; and then, from the vast and desolate darkness above, the weather broke.

ACKNOWLEDGEMENTS

Clay would not have been written without the following people:

The brilliant Kathy Gale (www.kgpublishingservices. co.uk), who told me I was a writer, and that I was writing a book; my agent Jenny Hewson at Rogers, Coleridge & White, who took a chance on something unformed; Robert Macfarlane and Jon McGregor, for their encouragement at an early stage; Michael Fishwick, Anna Simpson, Anya Rosenberg, Oliver Holden-Rea and everyone else at Bloomsbury; my sister Joelle, upon whom I inflicted an early draft; Joanna and Tom Ridge and Margaret and Tony Young, to whose homes I decamped to write; also Diana and Jim Elliott of Shillings Cottage in Hemyock; Magda Pukaluk and Wies Tondryk for help with the Polish language; Simon Wenzel of Watford School for Boys, for advice on school matters; Roy Vickery for his survey of plants on Tooting Common, and Roger Golding for information on ferns; Bianca Neumann at Veolia and Dave Oram and David Everett of the Lambeth Parks Service; the International Coalition to Protect the Polish Countryside; Mandy Barrow of Woodlands Junior School, Kent; John Enfield of the British Postmark Society. Despite all this help, any errors in this book are entirely my own.